Family Scars

Trae D. Johnson

Campania Publishing, LLC

2020 Edition

Publisher: **Campania Publishing, LLC**
Editor: **Dr. Melissa Caudle**
Cover Designer: **Rebecacovers**

Library of Congress Cataloging-in-Publication Data

Family Scars/ Trae D. Johnson

   p. cm.

      Family Scars/ Johnson, Trae D.

ISBN: 978-1-7355266-0-7

Printed in the United States of America.

Acknowledgment

As always, I want to Thank God for all of his blessings. Thank you, Father.

I want to thank my wonderful wife LaToya. Thank you for supporting this dream of mine of becoming an author.

Thank you, Dr. Melissa Caudle, for being my editor and blessing me with some of your wisdom.

Thank you, Rebecacovers, for your graphic designs. Thank you, Brittne Ballenger-Jackson, ESQ, for helping to format. Thank you, Lee Ashby Watts for your marketing tips.

Thank you to my focus group members Angela Duncan and A. Carolyn Edge. Thank you, Andrew Snorton for your support. Thank you, Chris Martin for your support.

Thank you, Dr. Corey Stayton, for your support and listening to some of the ideas I have for a plot.

Thank you to my father Jimmie Johnson, TaVonda and Robert Collins, Taryon Johnson, Sallie, and Preston "PAP" Bentley for your love.

Thank you to Virgil Dortch III, Eric D. Smith, David Reed, Tony Ellison, Melvin Frails, Quillie Hunt, Jr, and Eli Duvall. Love you guys like you are my blood brothers.

Thank you to Ken Love, Steve Yates, and Elliot Bell for your wisdom and for inspiring me. I want to say thank you also to author Brian W. Smith. Your writing and drive inspire me.

Thank you to all of my family, friends, book reviewers, and to everyone that purchased this book.

DEDICATION

I would like to dedicate this book to everyone who aspires to be an author. Let no one stop your dreams. I also would like to dedicate this book to my Mother, Essie L. Johnson, and my Granny, Moriah Johnson. Only God knows how much I miss you two.

With Love,

Trae D. Johnson

TABLE OF CONTENTS

Chapter One

12:30 p.m.

December 24, 2004

"Evelyn, Evelyn, Evelyn, Help! Evelyn!" screamed out Tasha, who on the floor tended to her mother.

Evelyn, the Assistant Manager at their family mortuary business, came to the house for a visit. She was downstairs in the kitchen, pouring herself a glass of sweet tea when she heard her little sister screaming out for her. Fear of the unknown, Evelyn rushed up the stairs as fast as she could. Forgetting that she was wearing high heel shoes and a pencil black skirt, she rushed into her parent's room and found Tasha on the floor holding their mother. With her nerves working overtime, without hesitation, Evelyn tore her stockings as she kneeled beside her mother.

"Mama! Can you hear me, Mama?" Evelyn pleaded.

She pulled out her cell phone, and as her hand trembled, she dialed 911. After giving the operator the address and requested information, she called her father who had just left the house for the post office. She let the phone ring two times and dropped it on the floor.

Gladys survived her first battle with cancer ten years ago, but was now fighting cancer once again. The second time it was lung cancer, and she had to have one of her lungs removed. Suffering from cancer caused Gladys to slip into a heavy spirit, no longer having the energy or drive to participate in activities that she enjoyed. The long walks with her girlfriends, going out to dance, or planting flowers were rocky tasks to perform and became a distant memory.

Evelyn bounced up from the floor, grabbed two pillows from the bed, and laid them down on the floor. Evelyn gently collected her mother from Tasha's arm and laid her head on the pillows. Tasha rose; eyes locked on her mother.

Working in the family mortuary business, both girls knew how to take care of a dead body and control their emotions, but nothing prepared them for trying to keep their mother alive.

"It will be alright, Mama! Just hang in their Mama. Just hang in there," Evelyn cried out while rubbing her hand.

Evelyn look toward Tasha, who was still in shock, staring down at their mother.

Tasha, who was the youngest child of Ellis and Gladys Hickman, came home for the weekend from mortuary school. She hoped to make her father proud of her by discussing how well she was doing in class and how she would like to do more for the family business, but like always, her father had other priorities that seemed more important than spending time with the family. In time, her attempts to capture his love were buried next to her painful emotion of feeling unworthy of seeing another day.

Tasha, unable to move, remained in disbelief because moments ago, she was heading to the bathroom to take out her weave from her hair and saw her mother from a distance listening to the oldies station on the radio. As always, her mother loved to dance, and if she saw one of her kids, she would insist that they dance with her.

After a minute of doing the twist and two stepping, Gladys sat on the edge of the bed, resting while Tasha walked into the bathroom. Noticing that there wasn't any tissue in the bathroom, Tasha walked out of the bathroom and saw her mother on the floor.

All of a sudden, red lights started beaming throughout the house.

"Let them in Tasha," Evelyn directed while trying to keep calm.

Tasha was paralyzed by the flashing lights; racing around in her mind, images of her mother alive and smiling, images of her mother in a metallic blue casket, images of life without her mother kept her frozen and cold.

"LET THEM IN NATASHA," yelled Evelyn, trying to remain calm as her emotions were all over the place.

Tasha stumbled backward, shook the nervousness out of her head, and hurried downstairs to let the EMS in.

Hearing a buzzing sound, Evelyn looked down and saw her father returning her call. Before he could say a word, Evelyn quickly shouted, "COME HOME NOW; MAMA IS GOING TO THE HOSPITAL, COME HOME DAD!" Then immediately hung up.

EMS swiftly entered the room. The sisters stood silently, side by side and watched the paramedics take their mother's vital signs and hoist her onto the gurney.

Evelyn and Tasha, still holding hands, watched as the EMS workers put their mother into the ambulance. Evelyn tried to be stoic like her father, and wanted to be strong for Tasha, who was now shaking uncontrollably.

As the paramedics put Gladys in the ambulance, Ellis pulled up in the driveway screeching in his truck to a halt, wearing a dark tailored suit, blue Armani shirt, and Kenneth Cole dress shoes. Ellis ran toward the ambulance as fast as he could. Before he even reached his destination, the mixture of sweat and cool water cologne gave a distinct and unpopular smell.

"I'm... I'm... I'm... about to get in," Ellis said while trying to catch his breath and composure.

One of the paramedics directed him where to sit, and then he gently grasped Gladys' hand. The other paramedic informed Evelyn and Tasha that they were going to Essie Memorial Hospital and shut the door.

Evelyn and Tasha were so caught up in the moment, that they didn't recognize some of their neighbors peeking through their windows and others standing on their porch, trying to look without staring.

Evelyn dug into her pockets, grabbed her keys, tossed them to Tasha, and went back into the house to make sure that the curtains were pulled, and the doors were locked. Tasha sat on the passenger's side and had already started Evelyn's car.

"Call Curtis, and let him know he needs to come home," Evelyn directed Tasha while they were pulling out of the driveway. Evelyn looked over at Tasha, who was still in panic mode, sitting there motionless, and breathing hard.

Evelyn grabbed her phone from her jacket pocket and looked for the last number that she could recall from her little brother. Evelyn hoped that his phone was not cut off, as it had been several times before when she tried calling him.

4

"This number has either been changed or been disconnected," the automatic voice machine stated.

"DANG IT! Who the hell can I call to reach this boy?"

Evelyn, who didn't care that she was driving ninety miles per hour in a fifty miles per hour speed zone, suddenly glanced over to her sister and aggressively pushed her so hard that her shoulder bump into the passenger side window.

"I need you, Tasha!" screamed Evelyn.

"Ouch!" yelled Tasha, while rubbing her shoulder and thankful that she locked her doors when she got in.

"How can we contact Curtis?"

Tasha pulled out her cell phone from her back pocket, "He called me last week from this two zero two area code. Let me see if I can find it."

Seconds later, Tasha found the number and dialed it.

A female voice pleasantly answered the phone.

"Hey, I'm Tasha Hickman, my brother is Curtis Hickman, and he called me from this number last week, by any chance is he around?" asked Tasha.

"Um, he just left, if I see him or hear from him, I'll surely tell him to call you," the female voice responded.

"Please do; tell him that our mother was rushed to the emergency room, and it doesn't look good. By the way, we are traveling, it looks like we are going to Essie Memorial Hospital."

"Oh my God! Yeah! I will let him know, no doubt."

Forty minutes later, Curtis walked into the house with a marijuana joint in his left hand and a black bag which held a pint of brown liquor.

"Hey Kyla, babe, you would not believe who I ran into at the store," said Curtis as he flopped down on the couch.

Kyla came running out the bathroom with her cell phone in her hand.

"You need to call your family!"

***

6:30 p.m.

December 24, 2004

Sitting in the waiting room, patiently awaiting answers from a doctor, the Hickman family and friends like Pastor Brian Houston and his wife Erica sat in the waiting area of the hospital.

Ellis Hickman, owner of Hickman Mortuary, the man that was known as cool and suave sat in the waiting room with his heart beating one hundred miles an hour, dreading being at the hospital, and not knowing his next move. Trying to avoid the thoughts of the worst possible news, he kept walking around talking with family, friends, nurses, kids, and anyone who would give him a moment to take his mind off of the now.

When people saw Ellis and Gladys, they were complimented on how they were such a beautiful couple and often asked what was the secret of a happy marriage?

Ellis would immediately respond by saying that his wife is his heart, and she inspired him to do better in life. When Ellis thought about starting his own business, Gladys was there to

6

encourage him to pursue it.

Gladys would normally struggle but eventually was strong enough to create a smile. Though she enjoyed the finance that came with the business, she missed the person who she fell in love with. Gladys wanted to go on trips as they discussed when they were dating.

Ellis would hear Gladys' request but felt that the business needed him more. As he waited for answers on his wife, regret waved at him that he didn't comply with her request.

Walking by the big glass mirror that showed cars coming and going from the hospital, Ellis stared. "Lord, help me, I don't know what to do, don't take Gladys, take me instead," he said silently to himself.

Ellis kept walking around the ER, hoping to ease his tension. And finally, he walked back toward the waiting room and sat. He gauged Tasha, who was in the corner, coping in her own special way.

Evelyn came back upstairs with a bag of food from the cafeteria. She handed her father a turkey sandwich, a fruit cup, and a bottled water.

Ellis looked up and smiled. The aroma of the food surely beat the smell of urine, ointment, and pine sol.

"At times, you remind me of so much like your mother."

Evelyn smiled while she handed a bag to her father. "Well, you know you're a diabetic, and you must eat," Evelyn responded.

Ellis looked over toward Tasha, who was still sitting in the corner, but this time with her sweatshirt hood over her head.

Ellis knew that he didn't have the best relationship with two of his kids. It was easy to deal with Evelyn because she took a liking to the family business, which made it easier to establish a bond. Curtis and Tasha, on the other hand, had issues that he tended to never focus on. Gladys used to remind him often about spending quality time with his kids, but that never seemed to interest him.

Feeling guilty, Ellis walked over toward Tasha and sat right beside her. He noticed that her bag, which contained a turkey sandwich and a fruit cup, hadn't been touched.

"You're not eating? You should eat." responded Ellis.

Tasha didn't respond nor look at her father. She kept her hood over her head and started leaning in the chair with her head lying on the wall. Feeling his hunger playing the piano on his ribs, Ellis started eating his turkey sandwich and sipping on his water.

Ellis was clamoring for the right words to say but didn't have a clue as to what to say or do.

"Maybe I can ask her about school," Ellis thought. Ellis turned his head toward Tasha and was about to say something, when Tasha looked up, quickly pulled her hood off, and her eyes widened like an inflated balloon.

"Hey Dad, hey Tasha!" a familiar voice announced.

Ellis turned his head up, disappointed of the person he saw in front of him, and their eyes touched but retracted like a negative and positive pole. Evelyn was right beside her brother, hugging his waist with her left arm.

"Curtis!" yelled Tasha while dashing toward her big brother.

Ellis hadn't seen nor spoken to his son in a year or two. Their last conversation was a heated debate that led Ellis to tell Curtis that he should get the hell out of his house and without hesitation Curtis left and never looked back. This broke Gladys' heart and brought tension among the family.

Besides the cancer, Ellis believed whole-heartedly that Curtis' behavior and action added to the pain his wife was suffering.

Ellis' last memory of Curtis is that he stood about 6'2'', 250 pounds, long nappy dreads that touched his shoulders, sparkling, shiny silver earrings in both ears, and always wore T-shirts, faded out blue jeans, and Air Force Ones. Now, he was shocked to see his 6'2", 220-pound son, with a low haircut, wearing a brown suit, white Oxford shirt, and brown Stacy Adams shoes.

Tasha jumped up and ran into her Curtis' arms like a one hundred-mile fastball to a catcher's glove.

Ellis sat there, without a care in the world, eating his sandwich, and he was about to take a swallow of his water, when he noticed Evelyn giving him the evil eye. He felt compelled to speak to his offspring. He took two more bites, then laid his sandwich down on the table and stood up to greet his son.

"Hey son," Ellis said with his arms opened wide.

"Dad," Curtis respectfully responded.

Both men embraced, but it was obvious to everyone, even the nurses on duty, that a cloud of tension existed that slowly moved in the room. The smell of marijuana scraped his nose, and Ellis backed up quickly, smiling, and trying not to draw too much attention.

"Have you eaten?" asked Ellis.

Curtis shook his head. "No. Once I got Tasha's message, I came down here as quick as I could." He gave Tasha a kiss on the forehead.

Curtis sat down, and Tasha opened up and spoke about what happened. Ellis became a little frustrated that Tasha never informed him of what happened at the house.

Looking at his son, Ellis wanted to ask Curtis how he was doing and why the change of appearance now, but he decided to be quiet knowing that one or two words from his mouth could ignite a fierce argument. The last time they spoke, it got so heated and Ellis believed that his son would have tried to hit him if he didn't have his gun by his side.

"Mr. Hickman," a man wearing a white coat with glasses and holding a chart announced while walking from the ER announced.

"Yes, I am Mr. Hickman," Ellis said while raising his hand to get his attention.

Evelyn, Curtis, and Tasha followed behind their father, hoping to get some positive answers about their mother while family and friends stood up and surrounded them.

"I'm Dr. Crawford; I've been checking on your wife, Gladys."

"How is, she Doctor?" asked Ellis.

Dr. Crawford walked up to Ellis, hands on his shoulder, staring at the pain in his eyes. "Right now, it's not looking good. Your wife had an asthma attack that caused her to stop breathing. We have her in ICU; she's in a slight coma."

"Can I at least see her please?" begged Ellis.

Dr. Crawford gave a smile and instructed Ellis to follow him. Without hesitation, Curtis stood beside his father like they were a tag team.

Not surprised by Curtis's action, Ellis said, "He's been a mama's boy since his first breast feeding,"

"She is connected to a ventilator to help her breathe easier," warned Dr. Crawford.

Shaking and patiently waiting for Dr. Crawford to open that door, Ellis pleaded, "I just want to see my wife, Dr. PLEASE."

Ellis turned. "Evelyn and Tasha, are you coming?"

Dr. Crawford informed Ellis that only two at a time could visit in the ICU.

"Just go," stated Evelyn while waving forward to her father and hugging on Tasha.

Dr. Crawford walked up to the door and clicked on the call button to be let in. Once the door opened, Ellis and Curtis followed behind Dr. Crawford like a child to a parent. Both father and son were nervous about what they might see but didn't want to show any weak emotions.

After walking past four rooms, Dr. Crawford pointed into the room, where Gladys lay peacefully in the hospital bed. Instead of a headboard and furniture, a machine clicked like a clock to keep her alive. Dr. Crawford opened up the fifth room on the left. Gladys had tubes running into her mouth and cords running in her veins, and her eyes were wide opened.

Curtis started panicking before he put one foot in the room. Twisting his head in disbelief, not believing that he was looking at his mother lying in a hospital bed, motionless, unable to say "Hey baby" to him, or to say she loved him.

Holding his heart and emotions, Ellis walked in with a smile. He bent over toward Gladys and kissed her on the forehead. Then he caressed her head.

"Hey baby," Ellis said while keeping his composure and trying to be a rock for his son.

Curtis stood outside of the door looking in. His nerves wouldn't allow him to enter.

Ellis looked back and saw how hard Curtis huffed and puffed. He was thankful that they were at the hospital in case he needed treatment.

After being in the room for about ten minutes, Ellis knew what was to come. It was hard for Ellis to fathom that he would have to make the hardest decision of his life. In the past, Gladys and Ellis spoke about if one of them were on life support, what they would prefer their family to do. Both knew it would be a tough decision that neither one of them wanted to make. He never fathomed that this question would confront him.

Dr. Crawford stood in the corner, quiet, observing the moment. Ellis looked back toward Curtis and started walking back outside.

"Hey, I'm about to leave. Do you want to see your mama? Are you ready to go?" Ellis asked.

Lips trembling, sweat pushing overtime, Curtis struggled to communicate but finally mustered up the nerves that he was ready to go. The pain of seeing his mother in this state crushed his heart.

Ellis nodded his head twice, and proceeded to walk back over to his wife, kissed her forehead, and whispered in her ear. "Words can't express how much I love you. Though at times, my actions don't show it. You are my heart, my inspiration, and I'm thankful for everything that you've done for me. Please forgive me for all that I've done wrong. I love you!"

After whispering into Gladys' ear, Ellis stood straight up and wiped the tears racing down his face. He looked over to Dr. Crawford, but didn't say a word, then walked outside. When he reached the door, Curtis was still in shock and pain. Ellis touched his son's shoulder, but Curtis pushed it off and walked out of the ICU. Ellis froze, watching him leave.

When the door opened, Curtis hurried down the hallway to the elevator, avoiding being seen by family and friends. His eyes filled with tears as he breathed rapidly.

Curtis tried to hold back the flood as he stood in front of the elevator with his head down and his hand over his mouth.

Every second waiting for the elevator door to open felt like an hour to Curtis. He kept pressing the down arrow button until he lost his patience and started punching the button.

Sis. Houston, the pastor's wife, witnessed Curtis' actions, volunteered to see about him. She walked over to him and slowly eased her arms over his waist and softly rubbed his back.

"Curtis, it will be alright now," Sis Houston said while hoping to console him.

Curtis started shaking and did not want to be bothered.

"It will be okay, trust in God. Trust in God!"

Curtis nodded his head in agreement but didn't care to hear anything about God. Through the years, his faith had been cracked.

The elevator door opened, and Curtis scampered inside.

"Please tell Evelyn to call me later on tonight. I'm going to be at the Riverwalk Motel and that she can call me back on that two zero two number."

Curtis grabbed his phone and started waving it.

Sis. Houston smiled, put her hands together in a prayer formation, and then tilted her head.

***

December 25, 2004

4:00 a.m.

Curtis lay motionless in the bed, staring at the ceiling. He thought about the last conversation that he had with his mother two nights ago.

"Mama, I think I did something crazy."

"What?"

"I may have fallen in love."

"You may have, or are you in love?"

"Um, I know I am."

"Good, you need a good woman in your life. You know I ain't going to be here forever."

14

"Don't say that, Mama."

"Curtis, I am at the point in my life that I can face my fears, and whatever direction the good Lord leads me."

"Well, I'm not ready to hear it."

"You need to; it's life. Matter of fact, I wish you and your daddy would start talking."

"Maybe one day, I'll talk to him."

"Hush! Don't disrespect your father!"

"Mama, I don't know if I can talk to him. He always thinks he's right, like he's God."

"He's still your dad, so respect him, he took care of you."

Immediately silence arose in the conversation.

"HELLO, HELLO... Curtis, you still there?"

"Um, yeah, I got a question, and I'm trying to figure out how to ask."

"Well, just ask, stop playing around."

"Is he really my father?"

Chiming noise from his cell phone quickly jolted him out of his daydream. Curtis wiped away the sweat from his face and then swallowed. He got up and grabbed his cell phone from the corner of the bed.

It was 4:25 in the morning. The only thought that came across Curtis' mind was one of the worst types of news that could happen to a family.

Curtis took a deep breath and then answered his phone.

"Hello... Hello."

Hard breathing roamed the line.

"Evelyn? Hey Evelyn! Evelyn. I can hear you crying. Is she..."

Ellis grabbed the phone. "Is this Curtis on the line," he asked.

"Hey Curtis, Um, Um, your mother has passed away," Ellis said in a low tone.

Curtis' eyes flooded with tears, and a cry deep from within his soul threatened to tear him in two. His mouth twisted open, but nothing came out, nothing moved. He was there but not there, lost in the darkness. Curtis was pressed against the floor, trying to get out from underneath the weight of the words that left him gray and then black.

When he came to, Curtis sat on the edge of the bed, trying not to think, hoping the thought he did not want to think was just a thought and not real, not a part of him forever, but it was there.

Curtis looked up, hoping to talk to God. He stared at the ceiling and started looking at the walls. It's been so long since he talked to God; he didn't know what words to say or how to say them. Suddenly his mouth motioned, and words fell like a waterfall.

"God, they say you don't do wrong. They say a man should trust you, but I gotta ask, why my mama had to die? She was a good woman. No, she wasn't perfect, but she was a good woman. Why did she have cancer? She survived it once, and then you had to give it to her again. There are people out there that deserved to die before her. What about the drug dealers, child molesters, rapists, or thieves, they are the ones that are hurting your children? Why her, why did it have to be her?"

Curtis fell back onto the bed, eyes pouring with tears, pain, and confusion.

Chapter Two

January 3, 2005

January 3, 2005, was the day that the world came to say goodbye to Gladys. Throughout the week, many people came by the house, called, texted, brought food, and even shared a good laugh with the family.

During the week, Ellis remained a strong man who struggled not to show his emotions in public. Behind closed doors, he locked himself in his bathroom, without the lights on, and waited for the sunrays to burst through the blinds while he sat on the floor. As a funeral home director and owner, it was one of the first rules that he learned. Behind closed doors, Ellis was a wreck. He was sleeping about one hour a night, sometimes he forgot to eat, and he would keep the lamp on at night so he could view the pictures of Gladys that he laid on her side of the bed.

Ellis knew that Gladys was the best thing in his life but never knew how much of a factor she really was to him and the others. Something as simple as choosing what attire to wear was difficult for Ellis. From suits, ties, dress shirts, T-shirts, shoes, socks, or blue jeans, Gladys used to pick out Ellis's clothes and laid them out for him for the day, not understanding the rules of color and what to wear or not. Since Gladys' passing, Ellis only wore a white T-shirt and the same black dress pants he had on when he was at the hospital. Ellis knew that those two colors matched.

After a week of witnessing her father's pattern, Evelyn started picking out clothes for him to wear. She was hesitant to ask him if he changed his underwear but decided that it would be too much to ask now.

The funeral home limousine arrived at 1:30 p.m. Gladys' body was already at the church for the people to view, and the funeral was scheduled to begin at two. The family exited the limousine and greeted the family and guests outside.

Pastor Houston walked outside to greet the family with inspirational words.

The family and the guests were instructed to form a line into the church, with Ellis being in the front.

While waiting to move into the church, Evelyn thought about all of her goals and dreams that she never accomplished, then wondered if that train of opportunity was too late for her to board. Turning around to check out the crowd that was behind them, Evelyn removed her dark shades and saw her little cousin Cheryl holding her seven-month-old baby.

Gently rubbing her stomach, *I wondered if he or she was here, would they have my eyes*, Evelyn said to herself.

Pastor Houston led the family into the church while reading a scripture in the Bible. Fellow Deacon, Eddie Crump, and his wife Carol escorted Ellis into the church. Troy Bell; Evelyn's boyfriend of eight years, escorted her, family friend Sheila Hampton escorted Tasha, and his lady, Kyla Levy, escorted Curtis into the church.

While many people's thoughts were on the family, many people were doing more gossiping, and head-turning over the girl Curtis brought into the church.

"Oh Lord, Jesus! The family should be embarrassed! With that short mini skirt, boots that go to her knees, and breast just hanging out like they wanted to give you a high five," whispered Trustee Hall to Sis Dent while the family walked up the aisle.

"Gladys was an honorable woman, and Curtis was raised up in the church. Why is he lowering his standards? Hell, I've seen prostitutes that dress better. If my granddaughter was single, I would introduce those two," gossiped Mother Turner to her fellow motherboard constituents.

Once every family member and friend viewed Gladys' body in the casket, two members of the funeral home staff came up the aisle and closed the casket.

Greater Moriah Baptist Church had never been so packed, as it was for the Homegoing Service for their beloved member, former Sunday School Teacher Gladys Hickman. At least eighty people were sitting down in the small Baptist church, with at least another twenty-five people standing up, and about nineteen people outside of the church that came out to give their final goodbyes.

Former classmates, former coworkers, girlfriends new and old, friends of the family, business associates, and church members all gave Gladys the utmost respect during their reflections.

"If you weren't Gladys' friend, then something was wrong with you," said Jerry Brooks, who was Gladys' first cousin on her daddy's side of the family.

"Gladys was just a beautiful person, inside and out, and yes, I'm heartbroken that she's gone, but I know that she's in a better place. I know God doesn't make any mistakes," said

Helen Bailey, the next-door neighbor, and Gladys' good friend for thirty years.

"There are things in life that are not meant for us to question, ask why, or get upset about. God has a plan. His plan was to take Sister Gladys home. A place we call Heaven, where there's no more pain and suffering. An' yes, it will take time for the pain to heal. An' yes, this family is grieving, and Hickman family, there's nothing wrong with crying, because Sister Gladys was a special person, she touched all of our lives here. I loved this woman, just as many of you out there," acknowledged Pastor Houston while giving his reflection.

After Pastor Houston finished giving his reflection of Gladys, he asked, "Is there another person who wants to share any reflections on Gladys?"

"I do, Pastor," a loud voice from the back spoke out.

Popping out of the crowd, strutting down the aisle like she was on a fashion show runway in Paris, Roxie Washington approached the pulpit to speak about Gladys.

"What the hell?" Curtis blurted out while looking at Evelyn.

For a second, Ellis looked up with confusion. The Hickman family began looking around at each other, with their eyes wondering what lie she was about to say.

"Is that the woman you said that owed your mother three thousand dollars for getting her son out of jail, and when asked when she would get her money back, she turned ghost," whispered Troy to Evelyn.

Evelyn nodded her head as she clenched her fist for the nerve of this woman today.

"Gladys and I were best friends. We used to go everywhere together until she fell ill. I'm going to miss our long talks, our chit chats, and the times we went shopping together. I'm going to miss her. She was like another sister. As someone said earlier, she was a beautiful person. When she needed any help, I had her back!"

"This heifer got the nerve to speak on my mama, and this woman owed my mama thousands to get her punk ass son out of jail," Curtis whispered to Kyla, forgetting that he was in church.

"Calm down, hey, just let it go," said Kyla while rubbing Curtis' hand. "God will take care of her! Don't focus on the past because it will only give you a dirty heart. A dirty heart is like a dirty rag…"

Before Kyla could finish her statement, Curtis pulled back a little; he was stunned to hear those Christian types of words from Kyla. This did not sound like the same street chick that he met three years ago who would have knocked out someone's teeth if they owed her five dollars.

Once Roxie finally sat down from her reflection on Gladys, Pastor Houston asked if the family wanted to say any words.

Throughout the funeral, Ellis stared at the powder blue coffin, with roses as its casket spray, surrounded by roses, peace lilies, and carnations, which were her favorite flowers. He wanted to say something and knew in his heart that he should, but it was hard even to mumble words to speak.

For a moment, it was quiet. Each family member looked at each other, seeing which one was going to say something. Sitting in the front row, Curtis stood up and turned to the onlookers. Pastor Houston stepped down from the pulpit to hand

Curtis the microphone. Inspired by his courage, Tasha and Evelyn slowly got up and stood by his side.

For a brief second, Ellis was impressed by the way his son took charge and brought his siblings on board.

Curtis turned around and stared at the coffin for a few seconds and then turned back around to face the congregation.

"I, I really don't know what to say. All I know is that when I needed someone, she was there. When I used to get picked on or got in trouble in school, Mama always supported me. She always had the right words to say! An' words can't express how much I love her."

Tasha and Evelyn leaned over to their brother, smiling, and happy that he spoke for the family.

Curtis turned around to face the casket, trying to fight back the tears, but testifying well on how great of a mother Gladys was. Tasha rubbed Curtis' back as he took a deep breath. One of the ushers came up the aisle and handed Evelyn a box of tissue.

Curtis turned back around and handed Tasha the mic. Before she could say one word, Ellis jumped up in front of her and requested the mic. Curtis was about to comment until Evelyn grabbed his hand and started squeezing it.

"When I first met Gladys, I'll admit, I was scared to talk to her. Um, she intimidated me. She was just a beautiful woman. I mean, any man would have loved to have her by his side. When I was first trying to get the scoop on this woman, one of my friends told me that I didn't have a shot because she was dating some guy who they say she was so crazy in love with. I was told that he was in the army. I told my friend that I could care less about this dude because I'm her future, and he is her past."

The congregation began giggling, and joy started to spread throughout the church.

"Well, I didn't know the guy, nor have I ever met him. I just knew that I wanted to be with her. I wanted to be Gladys Chambers' man. She had class and style, and I was just a poor country boy with a dream. Well, once she said yes to our first date, then that was the start of our beautiful life together. We just recently celebrated forty years of marriage. I'm a living witness; she has always been there for me, and now I'm just trying to figure out... figuring out how to live without her," Ellis said with a loud cry.

Many people were overtaken by the emotions that were shown by Ellis. Evelyn went over to hug her father while Curtis and Tasha just looked on. Deacon Crump and his wife rose from their seats and went to console Ellis. Evelyn took the microphone from him, and then he slowly sat back down. Curtis stood there, staring at his father in embarrassment.

As always, wanting to get all the attention and shine, Curtis thought to himself while watching his father.

Evelyn handed the microphone to Tasha.

"Yesterday was my birthday. I'm hurt that she can't see me, talk to me, or be at my graduation next year, it's not fair, I know God knows best, and maybe I'm being selfish, but I wish you were still here Mama," a tearful Tasha confessed.

Curtis embraced his sister, took the microphone, and kissed Tasha on her forehead while rubbing her back.

Evelyn was handed the microphone, "Don't give me my flowers when I'm dead, give them to me when I'm alive, so I can enjoy them. Don't tell me you love me when I'm gone, let me know now while I'm around, so I know how you feel. This was something that our mama taught us. Being a funeral director, I've seen people breakdown in front of the casket, wishing for the chance, that opportunity to tell their loved one that they loved them. But for us, while she was here, she knew that we loved and cherished her. And I can stand up here all day to speak about our mother, but she's in a better place. I have faith in God, and he doesn't make mistakes. I want to say again, on behalf of our family, thank you for your support, phone calls, and love."

Evelyn gave Pastor Houston the microphone, while Curtis and Tasha walked back to their seats.

The choir started singing *Amazing Grace*, Gladys' favorite song. Tasha's lips trembled as beads of sweat emerged as she remembered whenever this song was played at church, and her mother would stand up and started screaming THANK YOU LORD! She saw her dying mother lying on the bedroom floor, flashed before her eyes. Out of nowhere, her left leg shook, and the sweat started rushing. Cold. Hot. Flashes of light spinning. Her brain was on fire.

Two of the church ushers brought water and a fan for her. Evelyn got up from her seat and moved next to her sister to fan her with the obituary.

Curtis, whose head was down for most of the service, started daydreaming about his mother when Pastor Houston began preaching. He was still in pain and couldn't understand why she had to die. Kyla wrapped her arm around Curtis while he bent over and put both of his hands over his face.

Curtis could still hear his mother trying to tell him that he needed to get back into the church. He let off a cough and then put his hand over his mouth, and then Curtis pulled out a mint from his jacket pocket.

Before they rolled the casket outside of the church, Ellis stood up and asked to see his wife for the last time. Pastor Houston walked up and stood beside him.

The funeral usher opened up the casket and then moved to the side for Ellis. Pastor Houston got up from the pulpit and stood beside Ellis.

"Gladys was an angel, who touched many lives here on earth, I understand your pain, just as you will miss her, I will miss her. We all will miss her, but with God by your side, he will get you through this pain. Trust me, Deacon, I know," Pastor Houston reiterated to Ellis.

"I understand, Pastor, could I please have this moment alone with my wife," requested Ellis.

Pastor Houston smiled and moved a few steps back from Ellis.

"I love you; I love you, my sweet Gladys," uttered the words from Ellis toward his final viewing of his beloved wife.

Many people in the congregation started crying and wiping tears when they saw Ellis speaking to his wife in the casket. Even some of the staff members, who we trained, suddenly pulled out handkerchiefs and requested a box of tissues.

After six minutes of viewing Gladys for the last time, the choir sang another selection. Ellis finally nodded his head to signal that he was done. The funeral home staff closed the casket. Ellis stared at the coffin, tears running like a faucet, wishing he had another moment with her.

Pastor Houston came up behind Ellis to hand him a clean handkerchief to wipe his face.

Why the hell he acting like he loves her? Curtis was thinking to himself and wondering how long his father would keep acting like an asshole.

Sensing that something was not right, "Let it go," whispered Kyla.

The entire church stood in silence while watching the casket being escorted by six pallbearers, ten flower ladies, and Ellis Hickman leading his family outside to the cemetery.

Ellis, Tasha, Evelyn, Troy, Curtis, and Kyla sat side by side, in front of Gladys' eternal home, under the funeral home tent that was protecting them from the sun's ray.

Once Pastor Houston gave his final prayer, The Hickman family walked up to the casket and pulled a rose from the casket spray. They stood there watching the funeral workers begin to lower Gladys into the ground.

People formed a line to shake hands, hug, and offer condolences to the Hickman Family. Sister Helen McGahee began directing the family and congregation to the fellowship hall.

Curtis was happy to see some of his high school friends that were able to attend.

During the greetings at the cemetery, a mysterious tall, dark skin man, around 6'2", who wore a brown brim hat, navy suit, black shirt, and no tie walked up to Ellis and handed him a business card.

"If you ever need to talk, please give me a call," he

advised.

Ellis looked down, and the name on the card read, "Rufus Dennis, Support Service." Normally, Ellis would ask questions and be suspicious of those that he never met giving him a business card, but so many people were in line to speak with him, he nodded his head, smiled, and continued talking to the other people.

Afterward, the processional was in the church sanctuary. While everyone had gone to eat, Curtis walked outside and noticed that the limousine door was unlocked and with the tinted windows, was perfect for what he needed to do.

Looking around to make sure no one saw him, Curtis got in and pulled a flask out of his pocket.

"Dealing with this stuff here, I need this brown," said Curtis.

Curtis pulled out another mint and started sucking on it. Five minutes later, he saw Kyla walking outside. He got out of the limousine and walked toward her.

"Hey, baby, are you good?" asked Curtis.

"Yeah, now; I was looking for you. WAIT…you've been drinking," Kyla stepped back and stared at Curtis.

"Why you say that?" Curtis asked.

"Curtis, this is your mama's funeral. You should be there with your family, not with that brown or white or whatever you have on you," added Kyla, who was upset.

"You don't know my family. I got a father that believes he can do no wrong and a stuck-up-ass sister that follows her daddy like a puppy," answered Curtis.

"And now you're acting like an alcoholic son," Kyla responded.

Curtis stepped back, trying not to say what was really on his mind, knowing this wasn't the time or place for a full out argument. "Okay, okay, I'll go back."

"Before you do, go to the bathroom and wipe your face. If anyone asks, I'll say you were in the bathroom.

Without a response, Curtis headed back inside the church.

"Oh, I know that you mentioned that we were looking to leave tomorrow morning, but Evelyn asked if we could stay a little longer to at least have a family birthday dinner for Tasha."

"Um, let me think about that," responded Curtis.

On Curtis' mind was another sip of that brown, but he remembers he had already drank the little that remained of it.

Curtis went ahead and went straight to the bathroom. He bumped into his cousin Jerry while walking in.

Jerry got off the phone. "Hey Curtis, I got to go, Keisha's water broke, so I'm about to head to the hospital," acknowledged Jerry.

"Congrats, first grandchild?" noted Curtis.

"Yes, sir! Well, I know your dad is probably tired. Let him know what's going on and tell him when he gets a second to give me a call. I got some news for him."

"No problem. Tell Keisha congratulations from me,"

Curtis stated while watching Jerry jog to his car.

Curtis went into the bathroom and, for a moment, stared at the mirror. He splashed cold water in his face. He was confused, hurt, and barely recognized himself. "I got to get my life, right!"

Chapter Three

January 4, 2005

The day before Tasha got ready to head back to mortuary school, Evelyn thought it would be a great idea to have a family get-together for her birthday since she did not have a chance to celebrate her twenty-one years on earth.

Evelyn spoke to Curtis about the family get-together when he and Kyla came by the house after the funeral. Curtis was a bit hesitant in the beginning, not wanting anything to do with his father, but he knew how much Tasha looked up to him. Regardless of how he felt about his father, Curtis did not want to disappoint his little sister.

Evelyn mentioned the birthday get-together to her father this morning, who already had plans to just lay in the bed all day to moan, cry, and complain that Gladys was not there. Ellis even pulled all of the home phone cords from the wall and turned his cell phone off, so he could avoid the world. With a tidbit of persuasion and reminding Ellis that their mama would want him to move forward with his life, Ellis reluctantly agreed.

The family get-together was scheduled at 6:00 p.m. at Mario's Italian Restaurant. Troy was going to be late arriving. Evelyn came by the house around five to witness Tasha trying to get their dad ready to go.

Tasha removed all of the pictures of Gladys from the right side of the bed and put them back in their proper position.

Ellis was just getting out of the bed and was finally heading to the bathroom to take a shower.

When Evelyn walked into the room, Ellis' eyes followed her. "You know you walk just like your Mama."

"Thank you, Daddy, can you hurry up and shower please; I made reservations for six," responded Evelyn, who shook her head.

When asked about the family birthday get together initially, Tasha was not excited and would have preferred to celebrate with her newfound friends back at school. The drama was something that Tasha did not have to deal with back at school, and knowing her brother and father, the smallest thing would hit harder than a wrecking ball to a building.

Tasha hoped her father would not take his depression over her mother to another level again. After the funeral, Ellis kept repeating, "I wish that I had died first. Oh, I wish God would have taken me instead of Gladys."

Evelyn suggested to her father to seek a therapist to help cope with his wife's passing, but Ellis ignored that notion. Ellis got so bad with his moaning and wishing that he had died first, that when he went to visit Gladys grave, Evelyn and Troy secretly snatched all of the guns out of the house in fear that he may attempt to shoot himself, accidentally shoot Tasha, or someone else who may be visiting at the house. Ellis was so deep in misery; he lost his attention to details.

After waiting forty minutes of showering, Ellis stepped out of the bathroom with his clothes already laid out on his bed; thanks to Tasha and Evelyn.

Tasha was in the passenger seat, Ellis sat in the backseat,

while Evelyn drove them in her SUV to the restaurant. They finally arrived at Mario's Italian Restaurant at 6:35 p.m. Evelyn had already informed Curtis that they were going to be late.

Pulling up at the restaurant parking lot, Curtis and Kyla noticed Evelyn's SUV and started making their way out of Kyla's car.

"So, what do you know about her?" wondered Ellis while sitting back in the backseat.

"Dad..." responded Tasha, who was hoping he would be on his best behavior.

"Hey, I'm just asking, this may be your future sister-in-law. I mean, you don't have to really wait six or eight years to marry someone, do you," Ellis jokingly said while looking at Evelyn.

Tasha started looking over at Evelyn while chuckling over the remark.

Evelyn looked through her rearview mirror and gave her father the evil eye. In her heart, Evelyn wondered why Troy never popped the question, but she did not want any of her family members to be clowning him.

Ellis started eyeing Curtis like a boxer toward his opponent.

What a disappointment? Ran through Ellis' mind.

Suddenly, Ellis heard Gladys' voice like she was right beside him, telling him to spend time with the boy, stop yelling while giving him direction, and stop calling him stupid!

"A sad disappointment," Ellis mistakenly blurted out,

thinking he was talking to his wife!

Ellis snapped out of his trance and was confronted by silence in the car. "Oh, you heard me."

Before Tasha could respond, "Dad, stop it! Stop it! You keep saying that you love and miss Mama, but I can't tell by the way you're being so disrespectful to her son," Evelyn said.

Ellis just looked at Evelyn's eyes through the rearview mirror.

Ellis shook his head. *Only if I could have died first,* he silently said to himself.

Evelyn parked the car and turned her attention to the backseat.

Tasha got out of the car first, with the anticipation that something wrong would happen tonight.

"Dad, don't ruin this occasion by you and Curtis fussing," ordered Evelyn.

Ellis gave a sly, crooked smile and stepped out of the car.

"Hey, guys." Ellis walked toward Kyla, hugged her, and then surprisingly opened his arms wide and attempted to hug his son.

At first, Curtis didn't know what to expect, but he went with the moment. Ellis smelled the scent of marijuana and cologne on his clothes; he swiftly stepped back from the hug before the odor stuck to his clothes.

"Where's your boo?" Curtis asked.

"Troy should be here soon, he usually stays late to

answer any questions from his students," said Evelyn.

"What subject does he teach?" asked Kyla.

"College Algebra," responded Evelyn.

Evelyn went inside the restaurant to see if they could still get their reservation.

Curtis turned his direction to Tasha. "Baby girl, Happy Birthday, sweetie." Curtis, while hugging his sister, picked her up off the ground. Kyla stood behind Curtis with a card and a balloon in her hand that read, "Happy Birthday."

"This is from Kyla and me."

"Thank you." Tasha went over and gave Kyla a strong hug of gratitude.

Evelyn came back outside and was informed by the hostess that there would be a twenty-minute wait.

The family went inside to find a seat in the lobby.

"I believe I've been here before," said Ellis while scoping out the restaurant.

"They just built this restaurant here, you probably got it mixed up with another Italian restaurant," responded Tasha.

"No, I believe I took your mother here."

Evelyn cringed with a big ball of nervousness with the hope that her father would not begin to have a marathon talking about their mother.

The family found a seat in the corner of the lobby. While waiting, Ellis took a glance at Kyla and tried to figure her out.

He was so mentally out of it at the funeral that he did not pay her any attention at the funeral. One thing Ellis noticed was the way she rubbed on Curtis' knee and how she smiled at him. It reminded him of what Gladys used to do for him.

Ellis felt strange, not realizing that watching Kyla and Curtis automatically shifted his emotions to thinking about Gladys. Fidgeting in his seat, hoping that this feeling would stop, Ellis' emotions were going up and down like waves in the ocean.

Looking at his family, how bad Ellis wished that Gladys was here to enjoy this time with the family. He started smiling uncontrollably by the thought of Gladys's smile, which could brighten a room instantly; it could have made the sun jealous.

Ellis glanced at the floor, to hopefully stop the thoughts projecting throughout his head about his wife, but everything he saw reminded him of her.

Hearing loud footsteps coming closer, Ellis glanced up and saw a couple holding hands and exiting the restaurant. Before the couple reached the door, the guy jumped ahead of his date and opened it for her. Ellis stared at the couple through the large glass window entrance, and out of left field, the pain of not taking Gladys to Hawaii on their thirty-fifth wedding anniversary as she asked shattered his heart.

Ellis felt the moisture trying to develop in his eyes; he pulled out a handkerchief and pretended that he was about to sweat.

"Are you alright, Mr. Hickman?" Kyla asked.

"Oh yeah, I'm good; it's just a little hot in here," Ellis responded.

"Hot?" Curtis interjected.

Before Ellis could respond, three of Ellis' old friends saw him in the lobby and wanted to give their condolences on the loss of his wife.

Ellis thrived on the attention. His children sat back and watched him play his role.

"Yes, I'm moving on! I know God is with me! Yes, I know it takes time to heal this wound... Business is good, though we had a few people we had to postpone due to lack of funds! We buried three people this weekend!"

"Your daddy can be a good politician," said Kyla.

"Why, because he talks all that bull?" responded Curtis.

Kyla turned her neck in an angle toward Curtis, "They are much alike," she said to herself.

The hostess walked up and escorted them to their table. Evelyn signaled to her dad that it was time for them to get their seats.

Ellis raised his arm and pointed his index finger to his family while talking to his friends.

"Your father is very popular," said Kyla while sitting down at the table.

"I guess," Curtis responded.

"Our father has been in business for over thirty years, so beside him having a mouthpiece, he tries to help out around the community," said Evelyn.

"You still defending him?" questioned Curtis.

Evelyn gazed toward Curtis. "Don't you start." Evelyn

smiled as she gave Curtis the evil eye.

Ellis finally walked back to the family and sat between Tasha and Evelyn.

"This is a nice place; I wish your mama were here," mentioned Ellis while picking up the menu.

The waitress came by and took the drink orders. Ellis kept looking around the restaurant, and everything he saw had a taste of Gladys in it. From the carnation that the lady next to their table was holding the picture of the Chicken Parmesan meal, which was Gladys' favorite, to the lady walking with her date wearing nine-inch high heels. Gladys was addicted to shoes, and the waitress was wearing perfume, that Gladys dashed on from time to time.

"So Curtis, how are you?" Ellis reluctantly asked.

"I'm Okay!"

"You sure?"

"Yup."

The waitress came back and distributed their drink orders and began taking food orders. Evelyn got a call from Troy, who informed her that he was pulling up. Evelyn got up and met Troy in the lobby.

Troy and Evelyn came walking down to the table, holding hands, and Troy began greeting everyone at the table before he sat next to his girlfriend.

Unknowingly, Ellis and Curtis had the same feelings about Troy. Troy and Evelyn dated when they were in high school. Troy was Evelyn's first love. Both went on their separate ways after graduating and later found that connection that brought them back together. Maybe it was the guys that she dated, but Troy has always had a special place in her heart. Despite being reunited together for eight years, both Hickman men wondered why he hasn't proposed to Evelyn. Was Troy trying to get with Evelyn because of the family business? Was he hiding something? Both men never understood why he kept flipping careers. It was like he was so indecisive with his life choices. When he first met Evelyn, he was a Collections Manager, next was a Real Estate Agent, after that, a Claim Agent. Then he spoke about going back to school to be a Dietician, and now he teaches College Algebra at a local high school, which he claims that he loves, as he did with the other careers. What's the next job going to be, an MC?

Ellis turned to Kyla, who was interested in knowing the woman who had the key to his son's heart.

"Kyla, so where are you from, what do you do? You seem to make my son happy. I know if his mother was around, that would make her happy," rambled Ellis, who smiled, trying to pry information from Kyla.

Before Kyla could open her mouth, "Let me see, she's from Savannah, she's an Admission Rep for a college, she's twenty-five-years-old, and yeah, I know Mama would have loved her," interjected Curtis.

"Wow, that was awkward," mentioned Tasha.

"No, that was rude," Evelyn proclaimed.

Ellis looked at Kyla with a smile on his face and his hands interlocking on the table.

"Okay, Curtis, no need to be her bodyguard, I'm

assuming Kyla can talk," responded Ellis.

Kyla started giggling. Curtis glanced over toward his father, wondering what his father's next move was.

The waitress brought out the food, and Troy volunteered to pray over it. While everyone at the table had their eyes closed for prayer, Curtis kept his eyes wide opened. Ellis turned his plate counter-clock direction, and for a second, started staring at the food.

"Is there something wrong with the food Daddy?" Evelyn asked.

"No, this was one of your Mama's favorite foods, and I was just thinking about her," Ellis said with a shiny-gleam in his eyes.

Oh snap, Curtis thought while eating his spaghetti.

"Dad, we understand how you feel, but we're all grieving. Every one of us here! Mom would want us to be strong!" stated Evelyn.

"One day, when you are old enough to understand love, real love, you would understand how I'm feeling," Ellis responded.

Tasha started shaking her head, Ellis looked up, and without a saying a word, everyone's facial expression agreed with Tasha.

Ellis started eating his dinner, and among the conversation topics at the table were sports, music, school, and what's happening in the community.

Buzzzzzzzz.

Ellis looked down, and it was his cell phone ringing. It was his wife's cousin Jerry calling. He let the phone go straight to voicemail.

Ellis looked at Tasha and noticed her bracelet.

"I remember when your mom and I bought you that bracelet."

"Dad! Come on with the mama talk!" yelled Curtis, who was feeling frustrated, slammed his fork on the table.

Kyla began rubbing on Curtis' leg underneath the table.

Ellis looked at his son like he was a total stranger and Tasha, Kyla, Troy, and Evelyn felt the eyes from surrounding tables scoping them out.

Lowering his silverware, then wiping his mouth, Ellis paused for a moment, then turned his attention toward Curtis. "I think you better lower your tone, Curtis."

"Okay, guys, calm down, we got people looking at us, relax. This is not the time nor the place," stated Troy.

Tasha stopped eating and pushed her plate forward.

Curtis tilted his head, elbows on the table, thumbing the table with his right-hand middle finger. "Should I let it slide or not?"

Curtis felt his heart trembling and began to breathe hard like he just ran a marathon.

Like a dark cloud that hangs over, Evelyn felt the tension in the air. Curtis looked over toward Tasha, which helped calm his nerves.

"I'm sorry, Tasha," stated Curtis, who wanted his little sister to have a good birthday, despite their mother being deceased.

Tasha smiled and accepted his apology and then pull her plate right back in front of her. For about fifteen minutes, the family ate in silence.

Troy was trying to think of a good joke or good conversation starter but was too nervous and worried that he might say the wrong thing. He thought for a while and turned toward Evelyn. He could see himself marrying her, once he gets his life in order, but often wondered if he did decide to marry her, could he deal with her family?

"So, how was your food?" Troy asked Evelyn.

"It was okay, the sausage was not spicy enough."

"Do you want to take it back?" He asked. "Naw," Evelyn responded.

"It's kinda too late to take it back, she's about two bites away from finishing it," Curtis gave his opinion.

Tasha started smiling because she was thinking the same thing.

"Your Mama was like that if something was wrong with her food, she did not want to cause any issues, and just accepted it," Ellis intervened.

Tasha turned around to stare at her father.

Curtis started shaking his head in disbelief. "This Dude," While pointing his right index and middle finger toward his father.

Ellis slowly stopped chewing, quickly swallowed, as if horns from his forehead were sticking up, he used his fork to point directly to Curtis. "Is there a problem, Son!"

"You tell me," Curtis quickly responded. "Your daughter just asked if you could chill about talking about our mother, and you just did it again. We're all in pain now that mama is gone, but you keep on pushing it in our face. It's like you don't care how your kids feel. Just like at the funeral and everything else, it has to be all about you! It's always all about you!"

"Curtis, stop," yelled Evelyn, who could feel the stares on the back of her neck from neighboring tables.

Curtis turned his direction to Evelyn. "Stop it! Okay? Just stop!"

"Baby, let's go, Okay?" suggested Kyla.

Curtis was so frustrated with his dad that he didn't feel Kyla's warm, soft hand rubbing on his back to relax his tension that kept popping out.

Ellis raised his head. "Lord, why Gladys had to die, why couldn't it have been me? I don't know if I can deal with this headache."

Curtis stopped staring at Evelyn and saw Tasha had pushed her plate forward and laid her head with her hands covering her ears. Troy just sat there, turning his head one minute to Ellis, then the next to Curtis.

"Headache, you said headache," Curtis said while now focusing on Ellis.

"You claim that you love your family, but you don't know jack about us. Did you really love our mama, huh?"

"Now, you better watch your freaking mouth, boy!" Ellis proceeded to stand up until Evelyn grabbed him on the shoulder to pull him down. "Don't you ever say anything disrespectful about my wife and your mother! Do you hear me?"

Pointing and shaking his fingers toward his father, Curtis started giggling.

"No, Curtis!" Kyla yelled.

"Come on, guys, can we talk about this when we get home?" Evelyn asked.

Tasha stood up, threw her napkin on the floor, "I'll be outside, I can't deal with this," and proceeded toward the lobby.

Curtis started pointing in Ellis' direction, and then he turned his head toward Evelyn.

"Why, Evelyn? Why? Why do you always try to defend this man? Do you want to be in his will that bad? I mean, tell me? I mean, let us know," Curtis asked.

"Curtis, stop!" demanded Evelyn.

"Stop, huh? He didn't care about you. Hell, I remember when you despised this joker! Do your daddy realize that you still suffer from the fact that he forced you to get an abortion at age fifteen, and now since you're forty-three, you may not be able to conceive? Don't tell me you never think about it; well besides rubbing your belly."

Troy's mouth was wide opened; he turned his head toward Evelyn. With the corner of her eyes, she glanced at Troy, but never turned her head in his direction.

"Yeah, Troy, if you hit it, then you was supposed to be a

daddy, but ooooooh, we had to keep it a secret so my Deacon Daddy wouldn't be embarrassed."

"What? Is what he is saying true?" asked Troy.

Evelyn sat there shocked about what was transpiring.

Sweat started pouring off the top of Troy's head, while his eyes turned red. Kyla just sat there, shocked by the actions of her boyfriend.

Evelyn was speechless; she suddenly felt spurts of tears dripping from her face. She got up and ran into the bathroom.

Curtis got up and directed Kyla to do the same thing. Troy just sat in his seat, still in shock, wondering if the baby that she aborted was his.

"I think you need to leave before you get dragged out," ordered Ellis.

Curtis dug into his pockets and tossed out sixty dollars from his pocket and threw it on the table.

"This should cover me and Kyla's meal," Curtis declared.

The whispers, gestures, pointing, and reactions were the entertainment at the restaurant. Unknowingly, a few cell phones were already out.

"Let's go, Curtis," Kyla said while pulling Curtis' arm.

Four waiters and the manager approached the table.

"We need you to please pay and leave," the manager requested.

Curtis' eyes were locked on his father. Kyla moved Curtis five steps back, hoping to lead him back to the car, and then he jerked his hand away from Kyla.

With rage knocking at his heart, Curtis spoke, "Tell me Dad! You say that you loved Gladys... my mama! So let me ask you this, did you really love her? If so, why, oh why, at the age of thirteen, I saw you two arguing outside of your house, I saw you punch her in the face, and her falling back. I saw my mama in the bathroom trying to wipe her bloody lip. I saw her crying and in pain. She was in pain because the man that supposedly loved her hurt her. Right, almighty Ellis!"

Ellis slowly rose from his seat and started balling his hands into a fist as two of the waiters charged in front of Ellis before he could take one step to his son.

Curtis started gingerly walking away with Kyla attempting to pull him out to the car. Suddenly he stopped, and he turned around.

"Seeing mama hurt, and me, being too scared and shocked to do anything, haunts me, even 'til today, Dad. I wish I had the courage now, back then. You're burying everyone else. Hell, I can't wait 'til you die and go to Hell!"

"Leave now, sir!" the Manager demanded while pulling out his cell phone.

Ellis stood there like a mannequin.

"We are good; I said what I needed to say. I'm done, let's go, Kyla," Curtis said while walking out of the restaurant.

Ellis dropped down to his seat and began banging on the table with his right hand.

Evelyn came back to the table, reached for her purse, grabbed the little black folder with the receipt and the sixty dollars that Curtis threw on the table, and then gave the manager her credit card.

On the way home, Ellis kept moaning, complaining, and not knowing if he could explain his actions the day that he and Gladys had a huge fight.

"Oh, if Gladys were here, she would know what to do. Lord, why couldn't I just die first?" Ellis kept going on and on like a broken record.

Tasha hoped that Evelyn could drive a little faster, so she could go home and finish packing for school.

As always, Ellis was making like he was the victim and claiming that he didn't start any of the arguments or drama tonight.

Evelyn was hurt and embarrassed by her family's actions. Her last nerve that she had, her father had played it like a guitar.

Up ahead, they approached the Oconee Lake Bridge. Ellis kept moaning, then crying, then speaking negatively about Curtis and Kyla.

"Oh, if Gladys were here, she would know what to do. Lord, why couldn't I go first, why couldn't I go first, Oh Lord?" Curtis moaned.

Without hesitation or regard to her or Tasha's safety, in the middle of the highway, Evelyn slammed on the breaks and turned around toward her father. "Daddy, I love you, but if you want to die, just get out of the car and jump out! Just jump. Save us the heartache of crying over you because this is what you want to do," a furious Evelyn spoke.

Ellis just looked at his daughter with confusion.

"Take me home," Ellis demanded.

Evelyn grabbed the automatic stick and pushed it to drive while looking through her rearview mirror, then checking on Tasha, who was sitting on the passenger side with her arms folded, pocketbook on her lap, a stream running down her cheeks, and the look of hurt imprinted on her face.

While pulling up to the driveway to Ellis' house, Ellis didn't even wait for Evelyn to put the car in park before he hopped out the car without saying a word.

Ellis stomped up his driveway while trying to pull the house keys out of his pocket. When he finally reached the door, Ellis went inside without acknowledgment of his daughters, who were in the SUV watching his emotions go berserk.

This was such a bad idea, Tasha thought while still thinking of the disarray that happened at the restaurant.

Tasha, who had been quiet throughout the drive, hugged and kissed her sister. Usually, Evelyn would have words to say, but at that moment, words could not manifest out of her mouth.

"I'll call you before I leave in the morning," stated Tasha while opening the door and stepping out the SUV.

Evelyn gave a quick smile and watched her baby sister proceed to the house.

Evelyn watched Tasha while she walked in. Once she did, Evelyn was about to move the automatic manual stick to reverse, but she paused, and put her head over the steering wheel and started bellowing out an uncontrollable cry.

Not realizing the time or that Troy had been calling her for about ten minutes, she raised her head up and did not realize that she was at the same spot for about twenty-five minutes. She grabbed a box of tissue from her glove compartment and began wiping her eyes.

Evelyn put her blue tooth earpiece on and was headed back to her home.

"Maybe it's time for me to get away myself," she said to herself.

Chapter Four

March 2005

It's been two months since the fiasco at Mario's Italian Restaurant. Ellis couldn't tell you if Curtis was dead or alive, Tasha only called when she needed money, and Evelyn took control of directing the mortuary business; however, their weekly lunch dates became occasional events.

"God is going to get you through this pain Deacon," Pastor Houston always said when he popped up to visit Ellis at his house or the gravesite. Each day he left his pastoral office, walked to the grave, and proceeded to make comments on how the church missed Gladys' presence.

Since the day Gladys was buried, Ellis made it a point to visit her grave every day. It was like a new drug that he forced himself to take. Ellis gradually looked around her final resting place and made sure no ant beds or weeds overtook her grave. Often, he would look at the right side of the grave, and think that will be his future resting home as he continued to wish that he had gone before Gladys.

Ellis' normal morning routine was to wake up at 4:00 a.m. and stare at the moonlight while it waved back, saying good morning. Next, he caressed the pillow that Gladys used to sleep on and smelled the bedsheets that had not been washed since Gladys passed. Ellis smelled Gladys' scent that helped him to imagine that she was in the room with him. At 5: a.m. he finally mustered enough strength to get out of bed to shower, then find the attire that Evelyn picked for him to wear that day.

When 6:00 a.m. arrived, he strolled to his mailbox to pick up the local newspaper so he could read the obituaries to see what his competitors were doing or to see if he knew anyone who recently died.

Not understanding how to turn on a stove and microwave, at 7:15 a.m. he fixed cereal for his breakfast. Then, after finishing eating, at 7:30 a.m he called Evelyn for the latest updates on the business. By 8:15 a.m., he drove to the gravesite.

Looking in the mirror, Ellis couldn't figure out who he was. Many of his family and church members tried to encourage and help Ellis because they were scared that he might fall in a deep hole of depression. Some of the Deacons, along with the Pastor of the church, had an intervention with Ellis after church one Sunday. Ellis appreciated the concern and love from his fellow church members regarding him and his family, but Ellis denied that there were any issues and would appreciate it if they would stay out of his business.

Growing up in a single-family household in the 1950s, you quickly learned that hard work, dedication, and loyalty were the only way to survive. Before Ellis knew what love was, the only rock in his life was his mother and grandmother. His father was a well-known carpenter who was married and had a family of his own. Though many knew the secret, it was forbidden to discuss it. When life brings you lemons, you just have to figure out how to make lemonade; you just have to deal with it and keep it moving.

The father figure in his life was Mr. Brower, an old White man who helped the young Black make a little money. Mr. Brower ran his father's funeral home business, so when they needed help to dig up the graves, Ellis was one of the few that volunteered to work. Intrigued by the dead, Ellis began working for the funeral home at the age of eleven. Eventually, Mr. Brower took a liking to Ellis and taught him the business. Mr. Brower taught Ellis three principles.

First, to take pride in your appearance and image is everything. Mr. Brower bought Ellis his first black suit and shoes. Secondly, being sensitive is weak in the funeral home business. Those that mourn can cry; our jobs are to be strong for the families and give their loved ones a proper burial. Even when Mr. Brower's father passed, Ellis didn't see one drop of water dripping out of his eyes. Lastly, always handle your business. No one is going to take care of you better than yourself! Ellis worked hard, budgeted well, and went to school to get a license to be a mortician. Before Mr. Brower died, he told Ellis he would help him to obtain his own funeral home, but unfortunately, Mr. Brower died before he could make it a reality. Mr. Brower's kids knew of the promise that their father made to Ellis, but their jealousy of their relationship with their father and greed caused them to have amnesia.

**

March 12, 2005

Saturday morning, Ellis arrived at the gravesite and noticed a beautiful array of calla lilies on Gladys' grave. This was the third time in two months that flowers had been laid here. He meant to ask Evelyn if she purchased them, but it was never on his mind to ask her. Those that were close to Gladys knew that those were her favorite flowers.

While pulling weeds off around Gladys' grave, a white car slowly pulled up at the church parking lot. Around this time on Saturday morning, Ellis usually had the moment at the cemetery to himself; even the pastor didn't come to his office this time of the morning.

"I wonder who this is?" Ellis asked himself as he started back, pulling weeds and making sure the landscape around Gladys' grave was fine.

A mystery man stepped out of the car, and without shutting the door, started looking around the church with his hands on his hips. Soon, he spotted Ellis on the top of the hill.

Watching the mystery person's moves, "Morning?" Ellis yelled.

No response came from the mystery person. He stood gaping at Ellis like he was his prey.

Normally, Ellis would have his pistol in his truck or on him.

Still without a verbal response, this mystery person strode toward Ellis' direction. Ellis slowly retrieved his pocketknife, a country boy's favorite weapon.

Each step the mystery person made toward Ellis, his adrenaline of not knowing what's going to happen steadily moved up, up, and up.

Ellis had been in a few fights in his life, but that was about thirty-five years ago and even he wasn't sure if he could muster out the same strength as he used too.

This mystery person, who was now about ten yards from Ellis was looking right at him. Puzzled, like a game of chess, trying to figure out his next move.

"Morning, Ellis, right?" stated the mystery person, who smiled from cheek to cheek.

"Yes sir," Ellis responded with his pocketknife in his hand and blade ready to strike like a snake.

The mystery person was about to move forward with his hand reaching out but noticed the tip of the sharp blade targeting his chest. "No need for that, especially this time in the morning," responded the mystery man.

"Well, I don't know you! I said morning to you earlier, but you didn't respond. So, I can only go about what could or couldn't happen!"

"Can't blame ya," said the mystery man whose eyes remained focused on the blade.

"Hell, how things are going on with me now, if you're trying to take me out, I'm not going out without a fight; you understand me?" responded Ellis waiting on the mystery man to make his next move.

The mystery person chuckled and shook his head in agreement with arms spread out above his head.

"No sir, I'm sixty-years-old, I don't fight anymore. I leave it to these wanna be thugs in the streets to do that. I don't know if you remember me or not, my name is Rufus Dennis. I met you at your wife's funeral."

Ellis started twisting his lips to the side as his eyebrows lifted with confusion. "I'm sorry. That day I saw so many people that my mind wasn't focus."

Rufus slowly took his right hand, went into his pockets, and pulled one of his business cards out of his shirt pocket and put it up in the air so Ellis could see. "I gave you this at the funeral," said Rufus, who did not want Ellis to make any hasty move.

Ellis took one step forward, and Rufus handed him the card. "Okay, yeah! Yeah, I do remember the card, that day. I'll be honest; I don't know what I did with it," said Ellis, who used his thumb to put the blade back in its cravats while stepping back.

Relieved from the lowering of the blade, Rufus put his arms down with a high sigh of relief and then took a handkerchief out of his pocket and wiped his forehead and mouth.

"I do understand Ellis; I experienced that day myself. I lost my wife about ten years ago; so I can relate," responded Rufus.

"Yeah," Ellis said, who was bending over to pick out a weed that he missed.

"I know you have so many clients that you bury, but I did use your funeral home for my Anita. As a matter of fact, that's how I met your wife. I mean, my world just fell apart, but your wife helped me out, she even prayed with my daughter and myself. Ellis, your wife, inspired me to make a difference," Rufus said while walking up to the headstone.

Ellis flashed a smile and a head nod, but still wondered why he was here with him. "Yeah, she is one of a kind. My wife was a poet. She has a way with words that can ease anyone in distress. Many people from the church and those that lost love ones, loved her compassion."

Ellis rose and stood next to Rufus, feeling at ease and that there was not evil attention about to start.

Rufus noticed the calla lilies on the grave and some carnations. "So, where did you get those flowers from?" asked

Rufus.

"I believe my daughter purchased them," responded Ellis. Ellis noticed a weed that he missed on the corner of the headstone, and then he proceeded to pick it out the ground.

"I have a few kinfolks who were buried out here, from my daddy's side of the family. Since your wife's funeral, it has been years since I came out here," Rufus was saying while looking around the cemetery.

Ellis felt the vibrating of his cell phone in his pocket. He grabbed it and saw it was his cousin Jerry. *I'll call him back later*, he was thinking.

Ellis placed the cell phone back in his pocket and turned toward Rufus, who was still unaware of his attention.

"So, what brought you out here this morning?" Ellis asked, "I don't mean to be rude, but I was kind of having a private moment to myself."

"My apology Ellis," Rufus stated while holding his hands in front of him. "Truthfully, you," Rufus said while pointing at Ellis.

Ellis' eyebrows began to cringe with confusion while he slowly turned toward Rufus. "Excuse me. You don't know me to be asking for me."

"Yes, I don't know you as a person, but I do know and understand what you are feeling right now. And as a man who has been missing his wife for ten years, going on eleven years, this struggle is still hard for me. You don't have to be alone," Rufus passionately said.

"Are you a therapist," Ellis asked. "I ain't with that mess.

I don't need to talk to anyone unless you need us to bury a loved one. And if that's the case, since you used Hickman Mortuary before, you need to call the business line."

"No, sir, I am not a therapist! I just wanna be your friend," stated Rufus.

"I'm good! I have enough friends in my life. I had my church family to talk to me the other day like I was about to die. I got God in my life! We all have problems, and we all have a certain way to deal with it."

Rufus noticed that inch of denial on Ellis' face that wouldn't budge and a side of stubbornness that blinded him.

"God is good! But God also puts people in your life to touch you, to bless you, to help you out. And how hard you struggle to realize this, the harder each day will be to move on, and to finally live," Rufus explained.

Ellis glanced at Rufus for a second, and then turned his focus back to cleaning around Gladys grave.

"I appreciate you're wanting to help, but I'm okay, yes, I'm hurting! This storm will soon pass. Hell, this isn't my first rodeo.

Rufus smiled and shook his head with disappointment while he walked toward the front of the headstone. "You are a lucky man to have such a good woman by your side."

Ellis smiled. "That's the best thing you said since we talked."

Rufus glanced down at his watch. "Hey, it's about time for me to go." With his arms extended to shake Ellis' hand, Rufus stated, "Okay, if you feel that you don't need help, I can respect that. But I want to let you know two things. One, me and some other friends of mine will be meeting up at Highway Twenty-seven for breakfast in about thirty minutes. You are more than welcome to join us."

Ellis extended his arm and shook Rufus' hand. "Thank you for the invite. But I am good. I normally enjoy eating my cereal and reading the obituary... alone."

"Oh, seeing who you know that passed away," asked Rufus.

"Yup."

Rufus smiled and strolled toward his car.

"Oh, wait, Rufus! You said you had two things to let me know, what's the other?" asked Ellis.

Rufus stopped and slowly turned around. "When I was going through my pains, your wife prayed for me. We had a pretty good conversation. We talked about God, life, goals, and other stuff. She told me she had cancer, and one of the things that she was worried about was if she had died, who would look after you and the kids. And I guess you can say, I'm trying to do it now, as a thank you to her."

Rufus looked toward Ellis for a second, but words didn't spill out of Ellis' mouth. Rufus walked back to his car and drove away.

For a moment, Ellis was at a loss of words. Though he didn't want to admit it, those words from Rufus sounded like something that Gladys would say. She was such a caring person who took pride in looking after others instead of herself.

After cleaning as much as he could for the morning, Ellis

kneeled at the tombstone to kiss it before he left. Tempted to throw the calla lilies in the trash, Ellis left them alone but wrote a note to himself to ask Evelyn if she bought the plants.

Ellis got up, dusted his pants off, got in his truck, and left the cemetery. While driving, Ellis remembered that he needed to purchase some more cereal and milk. He stopped by the local supermarket and suddenly noticed Roxie Washington's car parked in the handicap parking spot. Roxie claimed that she was injured when she got in a minor fender-bender about five years ago, but many people felt that she was trying to milk the system, so she didn't have to walk so far when she parked.

"Lord, I hope she don't notice me."

Ellis ambled into the supermarket, looked in all directions to see if Roxie was around, then swiftly picked up a box of cereal. When looking to see if Roxie was in the aisle, he jumped at the opportunity to grab a gallon of milk.

Thinking he was safe, Ellis sighed in relief and headed toward the cashier.

"Ellis!!! Ellis Hickman!"

Ellis tried to ignore the fact that someone called his name until that person yelled louder. Ellis stopped and turned around, and he faced Teresa, Roxie's youngest and obnoxious sister.

"Hey, Mr. Ellis, how are you?" Teresa asked while walking toward Ellis.

Ellis tried his hardest to avoid her, but he was not expecting Teresa to be in the picture. "You don't have to yell," responded Ellis.

Teresa is another level of a headache. She was a

combination of a gold-digger, opportunist, seasonal victim of tragic situations, and the community news reporter on all the latest news and information in various neighborhoods.

"Hey, I just wanted to make sure you heard me. I know that you're getting up there in age," replied Teresa.

"And how old are you?" responded Ellis, trying to be cordial.

Teresa chuckled, then preceded to walk toward Ellis. Ellis moved back, not knowing Teresa's motive. He looked around to see if there was someone he knew if he needed to scream for help, but there was no one in the aisle but him and Teresa.

"Hey, come here, I'm trying to give you a hug." Teresa forcefully grabbed and pushed herself onto Ellis.

Shocked by this response, Ellis just stood wide-eyed.

"I am so sorry to hear about your wife. If you need anything, like a home-cooked meal, someone to talk to, or go out, please don't be scared to talk to me, okay, Ellis."

Although Ellis attempted to deal with his pain, he knew he was a target for women who wanted a man with money. Knowing that he was now a widower, gold-digging females may be looking to take advantage of his pain. And now, Teresa wanted to test those waters.

Ellis tried to think of a lie to get him out of the situation.

If someone sees Teresa holding him, in Ellis' point of view, they would definitely spread some type of rumor that he had moved on and forgotten about his wife and immediately moved on with Teresa. The thought of this petrified him to no end.

"Homecooked meal," said Ellis, hoping she would loosen up her grip with his joke.

Teresa looked up with a smile. Showing off her gold shiny tooth in the front of her mouth.

"Yeah, I can cook. Hell, I should have my own cooking show."

Lord, help me, Ellis thought. "Well, I got to go Teresa," Ellis said while gently pushing Teresa off him.

"Okay, it was good talking to you."

Ellis shook his head and powerwalked to the checkout counter.

"Wait!" demanded Teresa. Teresa dug into her purse. "I know I have one in here." She pulled out her business card and then stuffed it into Ellis' shirt pocket. "Call me."

Ellis shook his head again, and soon as he turned around, Teresa swiftly patted him on the butt!

Ellis jumped up with shock while patting himself on the butt like he was on fire as Teresa walked backward, smiling at Ellis.

Then she turned back around and swished her hips so hard it could give any man staring at her hips whiplash. "Something for you to remember me, call me now."

Ellis stood there for a second not believing what just happened. He pulled a handkerchief out of his back pocket and wiped the beads of sweat from his forehead. After paying for the cereal and milk, Ellis sat in his truck for a few minutes as if he needed to catch his breath. "Oh, for the love of Jesus! I can't believe that just happened. I can't believe she tried me."

Ellis turned the ignition and pulled off from the store. While driving home, Ellis saw Highway 27 Diner up ahead on the right-hand side and quickly noticed Rufus' car parked in the handicap parking spot. He pushed the accelerator a little too quickly, passed the diner, and then all of a sudden, a mysterious sound came flowing through the truck, "Go to the diner."

Thinking that the radio was on, Ellis reached over and grabbed the knob, but realized that the radio wasn't on.

"Go to the diner."

Without looking back to see if any cars were behind him, Ellis slammed on the brakes. Realizing he was in the middle of the street and not knowing when one of those Mac trucks would be coming soon, Ellis pulled into a gas station. "I know that I'm not going crazy."

Ellis looked up, and the diner was straight ahead. *Okay, I know I'm not going crazy. I know I didn't hear some voice telling me to go to some diner.*

Ellis turned his head and saw several people walking past the truck; he quickly turned the radio up so people would think he was singing instead of talking to himself.

For some strange reason something drew him in, but Ellis couldn't explain; it just feels like the right thing to do. He temporarily forgot that Teresa just violated him.

Ellis just sat in the truck and was bombarded with all types of emotions. One second he felt confused, then lost, slowly pain crept in, and then wondering what was his purpose in his life now.

Finally, one of his emotions won, Ellis backed his truck up, turned the radio off, then went back on the road and heading to Highway 27 Diner. "I don't know why I'm doing this."

Ellis parked his truck in the back of the diner. He slowly exited and glanced around to see if he recognized any of the cars in the parking lot beside Rufus' vehicle. A few seconds later, he saw Teresa drive past, talking on her cell phone, and shaking her head, which gave him much relief that she did not see him.

Ellis got out of his truck and immediately entered into Highway 27 Diner. Once he walked in, he looked around to see if he could find Rufus.

Before he could put the fork full of eggs in his mouth, Rufus had already seen Ellis while he parked his car. Rufus decided to meet Ellis at the entrance. Before Ellis opened the second entrance door, Rufus greeted with a big welcome. "Ellis," Rufus said while extending his arms.

"You don't have to be so loud," Ellis said while motioning his hand to let Rufus know to lower his voice.

Rufus walked up with a smile and then placed his hand on Ellis' shoulder.

"Um, I hope you didn't mind, I would kind of like to take you up on your offer for breakfast. I mean if you're not about to leave."

"No sir. I'm glad that you're here. Come follow me, our food just arrived but we usually here for an hour or two. Most of us are either retired or don't have to work on Saturday."

Ellis followed Rufus to a corner table where four

gentlemen listened to one loud guy tell a story.

"You can sit right here," Rufus said while directing Ellis.

Ellis didn't want to be rude while the guy told his story, so he sat down and listened.

"Yeah, I love these young ladies. Shoot, I had one to tell me that before I can mess with her, I need to get a doctor's appointment because her cookie, as they call it these days, could give me a heart attack. I was like woman; I pay too much for these Viagra pills to just not do anything with them. Hell, if I am going to fall out, let me get in a few good strokes before my time runs out."

The group of men laughed. Even Ellis started chuckling, something that he hasn't done in quite some time.

The loud guy turned to Ellis. "How are you doing, sir? My name is Maurice Walters." He was an older, dark-skinned fellow with a huge belly that looked to be around sixty.

Ellis nodded his head and shook his hand.

A young guy that looks to be in his early thirties stood up and walked toward Ellis. "Hey Mr. Ellis, I'm Carl Brown, nice meeting you."

A gentleman was sitting in the corner, with his "I Am Retired" hat on sipped his coffee. He waved to Ellis. "Hey, I'm Victor Campbell." Victor was a light-skinned gentleman with a long forehead, receding hair, and a gold tooth in the front of his mouth and was around sixty, give or take a few hard-worked years.

Ellis turned to his left and nodded at another man.

"Good Morning, I'm Dean Hunt, how are you?" asked Dean while shaking Ellis' hand. Dean was a brown-skinned man, with slick dark hair, wore black-rimmed glasses, and looked to be around his fifties.

"I'm okay; about as best I'd expect me to be, I reckon," Ellis responded.

Each of the men looked familiar, but Ellis didn't want to say anything.

The waitress walked up. "Is everything okay?" The waitress' nametag had Nancy engraved on it, but everyone at the table called her Sugar.

"Hey Sugar, could you please bring one more menu for my friend over there, and put his on my tab?" said Rufus.

"Oh, I got it; you don't have to do that," said Ellis, who never cared to let anyone pay for anything that he did.

"Nope, I insist," Rufus commanded. "I invited you. That's how things are done in these parts."

Ellis was about to respond until Sugar started rubbing his shoulders. "You good, sweetie; do Mr. Rufus gotcha? All I need you to do is to tell me what you want to drink?"

Ellis smiled and decided to follow directions. Rufus could tell that Ellis wasn't used to being told what to do.

"Sweet tea with lemon, please," answered Ellis.

"You had a nice homegoing service for your wife," said Dean.

"You were there?" Ellis said, who was surprised to hear

it.

"All of us were there," answered Rufus.

"We understand, at that moment, you were grieving and wanting to say your last goodbye," responded Corey.

"Yeah, it almost reminded me of my baby Tonia," Victor mentioned.

Ellis did not notice Sugar bringing the sweet tea and laying it on the table and was trying to take his order, but he was more in tune with examining the men sitting at the table.

Rufus took a bite of his bacon and then took two large sips of his coffee while silently checking on Ellis.

Ellis stayed quiet, not touching his sweet tea, listening to the conversation at the table.

"So, why the hell you guys were at my wife's funeral. I don't know you. I really don't know why I'm here," stated Ellis.

Rufus looked at Victor, and then Victor responded with a head nod.

Victor pulled out an envelope and passed it to Ellis.

"What's this?" Ellis asked when opening the envelope. He slowly pulled out a picture of an obituary.

"That's my Tonia," responded Victor. She's been gone for almost sixteen years, and no day goes by that she's not the first thought on my mind.

Ellis looked over the obituary. "She was very beautiful, like my Gladys."

Victor smiled and then took a drink of water. Ellis put the obituary back in the envelope, and Carl handed him another obituary program. Like he did with Victor's obituary, he looked at the picture and read the program. What made this different that she died when she was twenty-six.

"Wow, you're a young man, I'm sorry for your loss," responded Ellis.

A dash of a tear strolled down Carl's face while looking at his plate. "Thank you."

Rufus leaned over and rubbed Carl's back. Carl looked up toward Ellis, and with a somber voice said, "A drunk driver killed my wife while she was coming home from work."

Ellis looked down and suddenly realized that today was Carl's wife's third anniversary of her death.

The pain slowly kicked in Carl's spirit. Carl jumped up from the table, asked for a moment alone, and went outside to calm down and punch the walls.

Guilt poured over Ellis while he sat there thinking of all the good times that he and Gladys had, but there were moments that he wished he could have back to do more of the things she would have liked to do instead of focusing on himself.

The men sat silent for a moment. Carl returned calm and relaxed.

"Sorry, something just got to me," Carl stated.

"Naw, no need, we understand, today is not an easy day for you," Victor said.

Ellis was amazed at how strong Carl was. He wondered

could he have been that strong at his age to deal with the loss of his wife? Just to think that he never had gotten the chance to enjoy a lifetime with his wife, and he had a good woman for over thirty years, and at times he treated her like what she wanted never mattered.

A commercial strolled on the television above the counter about trips to Vegas and Hawaii. Ellis glanced at the television and then bowed his head.

"Gladys wanted us to go to Vegas and Hawaii, but I was too focused on the business to ever wanna go," Ellis said.

Ellis put both of his elbows on the table and hands over his eyes. The weight of missing Gladys, the troubles with his kids, and not knowing what to do in his life weighed heavy on him.

Sugar came by to take his order but a look from Victor signaled her to go back.

Ellis felt tears trying to come out, and he did his best to stop them, but like a ripped water hose, the pain flowed.

Chapter Five

After the restaurant melee, Evelyn called Troy that evening and explained to him the situation. She apologized for not letting him know about the abortion and not wanting to hurt him.

Knowing that he was supposed to be a dad, and Evelyn keeping secrets about it, led Troy into deep thoughts.

"I just wanted to knock his teeth down his throat," Troy mumbled to himself while thinking of Ellis on the drive home.

Troy slowly came into the realization that he wasn't ready to become a father, and terminating the child was the best decision. Although he wished he would have had a choice in the matter.

On the next day, Evelyn sat on her bed. Normally, on a Saturday, Evelyn would be in her office at the funeral home preparing her staff for the funerals that day; however, since they only had two funerals scheduled for the day, she decided to take the day off. Evelyn called Troy to see if he was able to come over to her father's house to help her box some of her mother's clothes.

Before Troy arrived, Evelyn had already boxed a few skirts, bras, stockings, pants suits, and shirts in Ellis' room. Evelyn searched for more items to donate.

"Wow, Mom, I knew you had style, but you got stuff in here that I hate to give away," Evelyn said while roaming in the closet.

The doorbell rang, and she looked outside and saw Troy's motorcycle parked out front. Evelyn walked downstairs to let her boyfriend in. "Hey, Baby."

Troy kissed Evelyn on the lips, and she moved to the side to allow him in.

"Troy... I should have told you. I'm sorry..."

"Wait! No need to explain Evelyn. So much I can say or ask, but it's not going to bring back anything from the past. So let's just move forward. Ok?

"But Troy..."

"Evelyn, let's move on."

"Ok."

Evelyn noticed Troy's silver helmet that he was carrying.

"So, you decided to ride the bike today."

"Yeah, the weather was nice, and I just had that itch to bring her back on the streets." He placed his keys into his pocket.

Troy dropped his helmet on the couch and then preceded upstairs to Ellis' room with Evelyn. "I got to say, your mom should have been a model." Troy rummaged through a few items that Evelyn placed on the bed.

"I wanted to wash those bedsheets, but daddy won't let me."

"What! These sheets haven't been touched. That's nasty!"

Evelyn nodded. "The perfume scent helps him move on,

I guess."

"I'm not going to touch that."

While Evelyn was looking through one side of the closet, Troy was about to start moving the boxes that were full into Evelyn's SUV until he noticed Gladys' charm bracelet on the dresser.

"Your mom's charm bracelet, I never understood it," Troy mentioned while picking up the bracelet.

Troy started examining the charm bracelet and admiring its uniqueness. The charm bracelet was all silver except a small key and cross that was both 14-karat gold.

For a second, Troy reminisced about Mrs. Hickman. Imagining her smile, her compassion, her way of making some feel important when they were down, never judging anyone, and especially how she can put her feet down in some peach cobbler.

Troy started daydreaming. Evelyn asked, "What do you mean?"

"Huh, what," Troy stated with confusion.

"You just said that you did not understand my mom's charm bracelet"

"Well look at it; everything is silver except for this key and this cross. Most charm bracelets are usually the same metal"

"I never realized that," Evelyn said, who just now admiring the features of the charm bracelet.

"My mother faithfully wore this charm bracelet, but I never paid any attention to this, until you just said that, wow."

"Oh well, to me, this symbolizes your mom and her style. She did things differently in a way that's hot," Troy said while picking up the box of clothes and preparing to go downstairs to load the truck up.

Evelyn shook her head and laid the charm bracelet back on the dresser and then went back to working on getting Gladys clothes out of the closet.

When Troy came back upstairs, Evelyn asked him could he take all of her boxes of shoes down? He nodded his head.

"Here's something else that I don't understand! Why you ladies need a thousand pairs of shoes?" Troy asked while looking through Gladys' closet.

"You can't just have one pair of black shoes, you got to have several so you can match it up with the right attire," Evelyn responded while smiling.

"You know you just gave me a bull crap answer."

Evelyn smiled. "Go do your job, Troy."

"Yes, master."

Troy reached for the stepladder that was in the corner, placed it inside the closet, stepped on top of the ladder, and attempted to grab as many shoes as he could.

"Dang, what's in this box?"

Troy carried three boxes as he attempted to tote another, but it was too heavy to move.

Troy went down the ladder, placed the boxes of shoes on the floor, and then went back up the ladder to wet his curiosity.

It took Troy both hands to pick up the box from the shelf, and then he carefully watched his step and placed the box on the bed.

Troy opened the box, and inside was a brown, wooden jewelry box. Troy motioned for Evelyn to come see.

Evelyn walked over to check it out.

"Have you seen this?" asked Troy.

"No," Evelyn replied.

"Check this out," Troy said when he picked the jewelry box up and wanted Evelyn to feel the weight in this box.

"This should be about five to six pounds."

Troy shook the box to guess what was inside. He looked up and saw Evelyn gave him an evil look, and then he laid the jewelry box down and looked around outside the box to see where they could open it.

Troy tried opening it, but he was unsuccessful.

Looking around the box, Evelyn noticed a small keyhole that resembles a heart on the bottom of the jewelry box.

"I wonder," Evelyn said to herself.

Evelyn turned around and started walking toward the dresser, picked up the charm bracelet, and grabbed the gold key, and just for curiosity's sake, she attempted to open the box through the small hole.

With a gentle twist to the right, the jewelry box opened! Troy opened the jewelry box that was full of folded up paper and notes inside.

Evelyn picked out a letter, opened it up, and began reading it to herself. Troy was waiting on her to tell him what the letter was about. After twenty seconds, Troy picked up a letter from inside the box, unfolded it, and began reading.

"Aww, this is a love letter," Evelyn said.

"Yeah, I'm reading all of this mushy stuff."

Evelyn gently pushed Troy on the shoulder.

"While others searched for their Mr. Right, I am thankful that I have you in my life," Evelyn read the first line out loud.

"That was so sweet! Why don't you write me poetry?" asked Evelyn.

"Well, I'm not as talented as your dad. I didn't know your dad was the romantic type," said Troy.

"Me either," responded Evelyn.

Troy tilted the jewelry box and dumped all the folded letters on the bed.

"I would love to show Dad this, but I don't know. He's not quite mentally right as of late.

While looking at the bottom of the jewelry box, Troy noticed a hidden compartment in the bottom. Not able to pull it up with his fingers, he pulled out his fingernail file, and used the edge to open up the bottom contraction.

Two folded envelopes lay hidden below. Troy took the envelopes, opened one, and read it.

Evelyn also continued reading over the love letters.

"Um, Evelyn, you may not want to tell your Dad about this," Troy suggested while rereading both of the letters.

"Why?"

"I found these letters in the bottom of the jewelry box, check this out," Troy suggested while handing the letters to Evelyn.

Evelyn read the first one, and then suddenly, she dropped onto the bed.

"I can't believe what I am reading. I mean, this is my mother's handwriting, why...why...why would she do this? I'm, I'm..." Evelyn tried to figure out the words to say.

Troy sat next to her on the bed, placing his arms around her.

Evelyn shrugged his arm off her shoulder. "There's just something's in life that we shouldn't know, and I wish I did not find these letters." She sat speechless taking deep breaths as her hands trembled. Slowly, she crumbled the letters and threw them at the wall. "What the hell?" yelled Evelyn. "Another man. My mother had an affair. How could she?"

Troy, in shock, didn't know how to respond.

Just seconds ago, they awed the love letters between Gladys and Ellis.

Chapter Six

Victor, Rufus, Carl, and Ellis left the diner full and satisfied. For Ellis, he felt more relieved than anything, which he still didn't understand why he decided to attend with Rufus and his friends. He never realized how much pain he had suppressed. As a funeral director, he was trained to know and understand how to deal with sadness when it comes to death, but this time around, he was in the driver's seat.

"Well, gentlemen, Lord's will, I will see you next Saturday," Carl said.

Before he walked off, he saluted Ellis with a military salute then walked away. Besides his demeanor, Ellis noticed the gun strapped on his ankle and knew he was a cop.

Ellis waved goodbye. Victor, walking with a cane, strutted to his car while Ellis and Rufus followed behind him to his corvette.

While walking, he turned his head and noticed a young man getting out of his car, then opening the door to the back seat, quickly picking up his son and placing him on the ground. After looking both ways, he held his son's hand, who looked to be around one to two years old. Ellis continued to watch them until they approached the door to the diner.

Memories of Ellis holding Curtis' hand came across his mind. Gladys always told him to spend time with that boy, but his mind was focused on the business. Deep in his heart, Ellis wished he had a better relationship with his only son.

For years, he imagined that he would hand his son the key to the business instead of Evelyn. Nothing was wrong with giving the company to Evelyn, but he wanted his son to pass it down to his son like Mr. Brower did for his kids, but hopefully, they wouldn't let the business go under.

"Hey!" yelled out, Victor. "We're over here."

Ellis snapped out of his trance and walked toward Victor and Rufus.

"Nice ride," Ellis acknowledged, while looking up and down at Victor's corvette.

"Thank you, sir. I got this last year for my birthday! I can't wait for summer, so I can drop the top off and holla at these young women."

Rufus busted out laughing and was happy to see Ellis showing a resemblance to being alive.

"Don't hurt yourself, old man," Rufus responded. "Too many of those blue pills can burst your heart!"

Ellis looked at his watch and was about to say his goodbyes until Victor asked, "Are you good and don't tell us some bull crap now?"

Thinking of the right words to say, Ellis responded, "If you could have the power to turn back the hands of time, would you, would you rewrite the things you should have done?"

Both men stood speechless for a second. For a brief moment, Rufus thought of that rainy day in South Carolina, when he and his wife argued and she ran out of the house, without a fight or stopping her for charging out the door.

"Naw!" responded Victor, who snapped Rufus from his brief trance.

"In life, we just have to deal with our decisions that we made. I can sit here for hours and go over all the things that I coulda, shoulda, I wish I coulda, but why? I just got to deal with the choices I made. Even if it's good or bad, it doesn't matter."

Ellis listened without saying a word. Rufus nodded his head in agreement, but added, "I agree, but if we have a chance now to re-write the wrong from our past, then why not."

"Amen to that!" said Ellis. He pondered about his family, and whether they could be on one accord.

Victor pulled out a cigarette, lit it, and puffed on it like he was giving it CPR. "So, what's on your mind, I saw you looking at the young man and his boy?"

Trying to change the subject, Ellis asked, "So how did you guys get this get together started?"

Victor took two more puffs and then tossed his cigarette in the street. "Hey, I got to go, I'm meeting someone for golf and I forgot my clubs at the house. I hope to see you next week." He extended his hand for a handshake.

"If nothing is on my schedule, I may try to come back," stated Ellis, who was still not sure of hanging out with the rest of the seniors.

Victor got in his car, turned it on, and then stepped on the accelerator; the car roared. "Sounds like a freaking lion, I love this!" He pulled off and then sped up in the street as smoke expelled from the exhaust pipes.

"I didn't want to say anything, but I hope he can handle

that power," Ellis stated.

"Ha, Ha, Ha. That's the same thing we were saying, but Victor can be as stubborn as a bull, so we chose just to say nothing," replied Rufus.

Rufus and Ellis stood there for a second. The sun became brighter, and the once predicted cloudy afternoon developed to be a beautiful sunny day.

"So, are you going to answer my question," replied Ellis.

Rufus grinned and then placed his hands on Ellis' shoulders. "We have more in common than you would imagine. The day my wife passed, well, you can imagine was the most terrifying day in my life. I swear I never felt so depressed in my life. My family tried their best to comfort me, but it wasn't the same. Ellis, I tell you, I couldn't wait for the good Lord to take me home. Well, a few years back, one day, while visiting family in South Georgia, I was watching the news, and I saw this report of this pregnant woman who was killed by a drunk driver."

"Whoa!"

"Yeah, and for some reason, that story just held on to me. I mean, I couldn't sleep or eat without thinking about it. It touched my spirit. I went to the funeral and met, well, you know Carl. At the repast, I pulled him to the side and just told him who I was, and I may not understand how he deals with pain, but I understand what he is dealing with in regard to the loss of a wife. So, we exchanged numbers and kept in contact. It seems like every day we talked. Things that he was just now going through, I knew and felt his pain."

"Okay."

"So, a thought occurred. Maybe there needs to be a

fellowship amongst widowers. And since there was not an official program, why not start it? So, where is the best place to find widow guys? Yes, at a funeral."

"Never thought about it like that," Ellis responded.

"And just think, the obituaries were our official map."

"I can see that," Ellis nodding his head.

"So, I started a new hobby; the hobby of seeing who's a male widower which was quite hard because most men don't outlive women. So, I started going to funerals, either giving them my business card or talking to them at the repast. A few men were offered to attend but declined the offer. Most were uncomfortable with sharing their issues with strangers. Those that came, well, we met up for breakfast. Later on, Carl moved up here."

"It was like a sign from God for you to start this group," stated Ellis.

"That maybe true Ellis. I never thought of it like that. We were our own therapists. Problems from dealing with insurance, annoying family members, trying to build back relationships with our kids, heck at times pushing our troublesome kids away, and the most common issue was women who were trying to get with us now for either money or convenience. Things that we never had to deal with when we were married, and now this is a brand-new chapter of our lives that we must live. And quite frankly, Ellis, it's scary!"

"Ain't that the truth!"

Chapter Seven

April 25, 2005

It was 3:45 a.m. and Curtis lay on the couch in the dark. He had finished texting and then set his phone onto his stomach. Today marked five months since his beloved mother received her heavenly wings. How hard he tried to battle his emotions, unsuccessfully, lost by a massive blow of reality that all he had left of his favorite girl were memories. As it did then, as it does now, the pain still stung. Tears poured, and Curtis didn't even bother to wipe his face anymore.

"I wish I could have seen her more. I wish I could have seen her more," he steadily repeated to himself. He wanted to blame his father, but deep inside, he knew that if he wanted to see his mother, he could have.

The very thought of her wanting his father and him to be on good terms emerged from the depths of his emotions. Curtis felt somewhat strange when he felt a slight bit of guilt for his actions at the restaurant.

Slowly, Curtis closed his eyes, and all of a sudden, he daydreamed about his mother -- happy times when he was a young man. From the time his mother taught him how to drive a car to the times she helped him with his homework, the flood of emotions erupted.

Curtis gradually emerged with a smile when his dream focused on a certain female. When Curtis was fourteen, he had a crush on Mya Murray. At that time, it seemed like everyone was in love with this girl. Back then, she was a caramel complexion, short cut Bob hairstyle like Halle Berry back in the days, five-feet tall, high cheekbones, and with hazel-green eyes. She started developing early, so naturally, her chest was a B, and her body was put together with perfection.

It was no surprise when Valentine's Day came the boys showered her with gifts. When it was her birthday, it felt like a national holiday at school. She didn't have to do much but smile. Gifts, flowers, cards, and balloons filled up the classroom.

While grocery shopping, Gladys and Curtis walked throughout the aisles headed toward aisle C to pick up some cereal until Curtis looked ahead, and then his legs came to a complete halt! Unaware that her child was not beside her, she kept walking until she called out his name. Without any response, she quickly turned around and saw Curtis standing at the entrance of the aisle like he was cemented at that spot. Gladys looked over and saw Mya and her mother strolling through the other side aisle.

Smiling, Evelyn kept on shopping for cereal and any other items they may need.

Most guys would have taken that chance to say hello and be smooth around her; however, Curtis remained idle. When Mya and her mother left, Curtis seemed to melt away the fear and come back into reality. Gladys couldn't help but laugh to herself.

It was evident to Gladys that this girl had a hold on her son. She was happy that he had a little crush on a pretty, young girl, but knowing that eventually, her son would like to start talking to women and then finally start taking them out on dates, she knew she had to prep her son on girls. Gladys couldn't have her only son being someone's sugar daddy or worse, a sucker.

On the drive home, Gladys was curious to get Curtis' view of why he kept moving around the aisle.

Curtis tried to play cool, "I just wanted to make sure we didn't miss anything," he responded.

Gladys grinned. *Aww, that was so cute.* "I thought you were too nervous to speak to that pretty girl at the store."

"Nervous? Naw, I'm too smooth for that, Mama," Curtis responded, rubbing his hands on his knees.

Gladys stopped at the red light and then turned her head toward Curtis, who was squirming all around his seat. "Well, I know that this is a conversation that you should be having with your father, but since he's at work, if you ever want advice on how to talk to girls, well, since I was once a teenage girl, maybe I can give you some pointers."

The light turned green, and Gladys proceeded to head home. Gladys turned up the radio until she felt the bass from the speakers and began singing. Curtis was on the passenger side, silent, but listening to the radio.

"When you say how to talk to girls, do you mean having them to like you?"

Gladys turned down the radio and asked Curtis to repeat what he said. Once he did, she thought for a second of what should she say next. Once she configured her words, she was ready to break it down. "Well, a pretty girl like that, I can imagine she has all the boys wanting her."

Curtis nodded his head. "She does have a lot of admirers."

"Well, you may not like this Curtis, but your next

obstacle is that you need to ignore her."

"Huh?"

Gladys stopped at the next red light. She turned her head and this time, Curtis was staring right back at her.

"When I say ignore her, what I mean is that if every little boy is trying to talk to her, they are spoiling her. See, you don't want to be like those other boys. You got to do something that stands out. If you or anybody else tries to step up to her, you will be just another notch on her belt. You would have to be super popular to get her attention enough to say screw everybody else. But... if you ignore her, start being super nice to all the other women, I guarantee you that they will speak your name so much that you will be the boy of the month. Then she would get jealous because she would think that she got all the boys wrapped up around her finger, except for you! And for any girl, that would drive her crazy because she would simply like a challenge."

Curtis absorbed all of the knowledge that his mother just gave him trying to figure out how he should start.

"And Curtis, there is one more thing that you must do, if you can get this, you can probably have any girl you like."

"What Mama?"

"You must do great in your schoolwork!"

"Huh, I do, Okay?"

"No, you need to change from being just a C student to an A-plus. Curtis, she is a pretty girl. And being pretty, people will let you get away with things. Unfortunately, if you're pretty enough, they will just let you slide by. But once in a while, girls like her will have to deal with a situation that their looks, or popularity cannot help them with. I guarantee you that if you do well in your class, and she knows you're good at a subject, she will be coming after you for help. And all you need to do is give her the one-on-one attention for her studies, make sure that she is comfortable, because at the moment she would be vulnerable. You can be a good influence on her, and when she does well on the subject, then she will thank you."

Curtis looked up to his mother, then stared straight ahead, with his hand over his head. "Okay, let's see if this plan is going to work."

Curtis made a drastic change. Normally after school, he headed straight to the park to play basketball, but today he chose to stay home and complete all of his assignments and read further chapters for school. He was so focused on his school assignments that anyone could have sworn that he was trying to get into an Ivy League school like Yale and Harvard. At school, though he was tempted to stare and fantasize over Mya, he wholly followed his mother's advice and ignored her and focused on being nice to the other young ladies, which word quickly spread around.

Mr. Burrus, Curtis' algebra teacher, informed the class of their midterm exam. With Curtis' new renewed love for education, he had the highest grade in the class. Mr. Burrus started passing out last week's pop quiz. Curtis, as usual, made an A. Sitting in the front row was Mya. Mr. Burrus handed her the pop quiz, and suddenly she turned over the paper and put her hands over her face.

The bell rang and all the students got their belongings and headed to their next class. Mya took her hands off her face and remained seated. While Curtis walked up the aisle to leave, he saw some of Mya's friends walk to her desk. Not trying to pay them no attention, Curtis kept walking toward the door.

"Curtis!" someone called his name.

Curtis turned around and surprisingly saw Mya waving him back toward her. Trying to be poised, Curtis moved out the way from the students behind him and walked to Mya. Her friends walked away once Curtis came back.

"Hey, Curtis, you're good at this algebra stuff, right?" asked Mya.

"Yeah, I'm okay," Curtis responded, with both hands in his pockets, trying to avoid smiling, while feeling a sudden growth spurt.

"I need help! See, I got a sixty on this pop quiz. I suck in this class!"

Slowly Curtis started breathing out of his mouth.

"If I do not pass this class, then I won't be able to stay on the cheerleading squad. Could you help me?"

"Yeah, I don't mind helping out," responded Curtis.

"Oh, great." Mya tore out a piece of paper from her notebook and wrote her phone number down. "Please, please, please, call me tonight so we can plan something."

Curtis stood there marveled in the moment. Many days he dreamed of asking for Mya's number, and right now, this second, he didn't have to ask; she gave it up willingly.

"Cool." Curtis took his moist hand out of his pocket to reach for the number, wondering if she noticed it.

Mya got out of her seat, feeling relieved that she had someone to tutor her, and started walking out the door. Curtis stood there in disbelief. Later that night, Curtis called her, and they both agreed to meet up this weekend at the library.

Before heading to the library, Gladys gave Curtis some tips on how to work the study date to his advantage. "One, focus on the math problem and see what her weakness is. Two, stay focused and make sure that you do several problems until she gets it. Three, take a short break like ten minutes. Within that time, she would be frustrated or relieved; either way she would feel more comfortable toward you about opening up. Finally, do not leave the library until she finally understands the assignment. Got it?"

On the day of the midterm exam, Mya stated that she was nervous but ready. Curtis had already told her how proud he was and believed that she would do well. A week later, Mr. Burrus finished grading the midterms and passed the graded papers to the class. Curtis received his paper but didn't bother to look at it because his attention was on Mya.

Mr. Burrus placed her test on her desk, and at first, she was hesitant, but she slowly turned over the paper. "Yeah!" screamed Mya. She turned around and gave Curtis a thumbs up.

Mya and Curtis met up after class. She was so thrilled to make a B on the midterm final. Curtis was calm and cool until Mya offered to take him out to the movies to show him her appreciation.

That moment taught Curtis to live by every word his mother said.

Just as excited about thinking of the great times, his daydream turned dark, and the image of his father surfaced. Curtis started twisting around the couch until his cell phone slipped into one of the cracks in the back of the sofa.

Curtis popped up from the couch and was greeted with Kyla staring at him in a lit room. Curtis was dazed, panicking, cold, and angry at what he saw.

"Baby, you alright, do you need some water," Kyla asked.

"Yeah, if you don't mind," responded Curtis while moving himself up from the couch. He wiped his eyes with his shirt.

"That must have been a heck of dream."

"More of a nightmare."

"What was it about? Was it about your mother?"

"It's nothing! Just give me the water, Ok. And why are you up anyway?" asked Curtis who was trying to change the subject.

Kyla bypassed Curtis' stretched out hand for the cup of water and immediately slammed it on the wooden coffee table. Curtis looked down and noticed the chipped wood from the cup meeting the table that was a result of Kyla's attitude.

"What the...!"

Kyla glanced at Curtis, then stormed back into the bedroom.

Curtis leaned back on the couch, with his arms stretched out in the air, without a thought he punched the armrest. Staring in the direction of the bedroom, Curtis jumped up from the couch.

Kyla was on her side of the bed, with covers covering

her head, relaxing on top of two pillows. Curtis went to his side, pulled up the covers, and slid right into bed. He lay right next to Kyla, hoping to wrap his arms around her so he can cuddle with her.

Instinctively she knew he was there and moved a few inches away from him.

Curtis would admit if he were wrong; however, if he firmly believed that he was right, like his father, which he never admitted, he would argue and debate until he proves his point. Lying next to Kyla, he was in a ball of confusion by her actions. All he was expecting was a cup of water, not an attitude.

"Kyla, what's going on? What's up with that slamming the cup down? You just chipped the table." Curtis huffed frustrated.

Kyla, under the covers, refused to respond.

Curtis, tempted to ask another question, looked at the clock and decided not to. "I ain't in the mood to deal with this silent treatment!" He laid his head on the pillow and attempted to go to sleep.

Kyla pulled the covers off her head, back toward Curtis.

"We used to talk. And yes, there are things that you choose not to tell me which I never really sweat you about. But lately, you've been acting funny. Like you don't wanna talk to me about anything. Hell, I was sleeping good, until I heard you screaming. And when I asked about your dream, you pushed me away. Like you are mad at me. So I just said screw you!"

Curtis lay there in silence, eyes closed, absorbing all that Kyla just said. Inside, he felt remorseful of his behavior toward her. When the world was against him, from day one, she stood by him, and never looked back.

"My father and I never saw eye to eye. Well, it seems like no one in the household did, but my mom stayed and was supportive. If she had the courage, she would probably have left him a long time ago. But who knows, he had the money to take care of her treatment. He was a well-respected businessman, deacon of the church, and how would that look to the people that his wife left him? He was more focused on his business than his family. And when he did come home, he was a dictator. Hell, I truly believe that he thought he was Jesus Christ. Evelyn and Tasha always tried to win their father's love. Evelyn wild out one night, got pregnant, and was forced to get an abortion. I remember hearing mama trying to convince him to keep the baby. But... like always, it was about him, and he didn't want his image ruined. I guess since she fell from daddy's grace, she took on the mortuary business to get his love back. Evelyn always wanted to be a dancer, that's what she always talked about! And for Tasha, he would never give her the love she desired as a father. So many times, she wanted him there, but he turned a blind eye, and I was like the father in her life. When Tasha wanted to learn how to ride a bike, I taught her. When her first crush broke her heart, I was there to listen to her cries. When she wanted to go to the father-daughter dance, he told her that he was too busy, but I took her out to the movies that night so she could ease the pain of our father. And when we came back home that evening, he was at the kitchen table eating banana pudding. Eating Banana pudding was more important than spending quality time with his baby girl. He is a poor excuse for a man."

Kyla turned around and placed her arm around Curtis. The light from the moon reflected down in the bedroom which clearly showed the red of hate in Curtis' eyes.

"Since you were his only son, was he expecting you to take over the business?" asked Kyla.

"I believe so!"

Kyla began rubbing Curtis' chest.

"I wouldn't mind being in the business, but dealing with him, I rather not touch it!"

"I understand that you don't see eye to eye with your dad, but is there any particular issue that still haunts you?"

Curtis took a deep breath and then glanced at the moon.

"Growing up, if my parents had a dispute, they would tell us to go outside to play or go downstairs while they go in their rooms, lock the door, put the TV on, and handle their business. It wasn't until a few years ago when Mama told us that they never wanted us to see them squabble."

Kyla stopped rubbing his chest. "We did the same thing."

"Of course, when we got older, the naïve kids knew that something wasn't right when every other day we were sent to our rooms. Heck, with school, and the mortuary business, we never saw our parents together in one spot for more than an hour. I know for Evelyn and I, we had a feeling that something wasn't right."

Tired of lying on his back, Curtis got up and sat on the edge of the bed.

"One day, when they told us to play outside, I saw my dad walking outside to his car. He didn't even look in our direction. I went back inside the house to use the restroom. I sat on the stall for a few seconds, and then moments after, I heard my father's size thirteen footsteps marching up the hallway toward the bedroom."

Curtis paused with his head down. He stood up and walks toward the window. Kyla laid on her side, gripping her pillow.

"I sat there quietly, but I had somewhat of a sick feeling. The door yanked opened and how hard he slammed the door sounded like two cars meeting head on. And what I heard next, I couldn't believe, especially coming from this well-respected Christian man!"

Curtis turned around.

"He called my mother, his wife, that he proclaimed that he loved a dumb whore."

Kyla's eyes grew like a balloon being blown up. The man that she believed was heartbroken, and a sweet man was using inimical words to describe his wife.

"Oh my God," Kyla responded.

Curtis sat back down on the edge of the bed.

"Yeah. I was scared. I didn't want anything to happen to my Mama. I wanted to do something, but I was a kid. I stayed in the bathroom until I heard him walking back down the hallway."

"Oh Curtis. That's understandable. What happened next?"

"Well, after I was finished, I opened the door and checked to see if my old man was coming back up. When things felt safe, I tiptoed into my parents' room to see how my mother was, since she still hadn't come out. I wasn't in my parents' bedroom yet, and I could hear the cries coming out of the bathroom. Hearing my mother crying brought a certain rage that I never felt before. It was like hate; hate that I never felt before that was aimed at my father. The phone rang, and my mother picked it up and she went into the bathroom within their room. She shut the door and I tiptoed into the bedroom. She answered and said, 'I'm alright, I'm okay. Yes, I am good. If I needed to leave, I would, okay. I tried to remain very quiet."

Kyla got up onto her knees and laid her chest on Curtis' back while caressing him and then kissed him on his neck. She knew this was tough for him to discuss, and she was honored for him to open up about this ordeal.

"I stood still while listening to her conversation. I couldn't swallow nor blink! Then without warning, I heard my father coming back up the hallway, shaking the ground with his stomps. Knowing that I shouldn't be there, I thought fast about what I should do. I rushed under their bed and tried to breathe slowly so no one would hear me. I looked up and saw my father's size thirteen black shoes smashing the rug. 'Yeah, he may not be the father,' Mama said tearfully. I tried to comprehend that thought. I guess my mom didn't hear him, and I couldn't warn her."

"What! You're telling all of our business to one of your nosey-ass girlfriends. I betcha its Sheena; yeah, it's probably her! I don't like that heifer anyway! And I may not be the father, what the hell were you thinking? I heard him grab the doorknob and trying to open it, but Mama locked it. I saw my dad's legs took three steps back, and then he quickly stepped two steps forward and used his left leg to kick the knob off the hinges. He quickly opened the door and pulled my mother out."

"That must've been traumatic."

"Very! My heart was beating in milli-seconds. I felt like oxygen was being vacuumed out of me. I was so scared that I just pissed on myself! Not a little squirt. I was hoping that neither of them could smell it. Then I heard a pop like it came from a ball bursting. Then my Mama fell back on the floor. She lay there, holding her mouth while my dad kept cursing. I saw a drop of blood run down her cheek. I was petrified! I lay there motionless, which I'm glad, cause if I had said anything, I wouldn't know what to do. My Mom turned her head and saw me hiding under the bed, and then quickly, she just looked up toward my dad."

"Definitely traumatic. I'm sorry, Curtis you had to go through this. No child should."

"My head was spinning and was about to tumble. I didn't know what to expect! That moment was so unreal that I was like a statue, and my eyes were fixated on that moment. Then the doorbell rang. I watched my father's shoes glide to the window to see whose car was out there. 'Dang it! That's Pastor. Why the hell he just don't call before he comes.' my Dad said. He wanted him to leave but kinda figured that Evelyn probably told him that he was home. Then Dad raced to the bathroom, I heard water running, which I'm assuming that he was wiping his face, and then he went down to greet Pastor."

"Curtis, I don't know what to say."

"No need. After he left, Mama went into the bathroom. I slowly crawled out from under the bed. I began looking up and down at the bathroom door, and then I glanced at my Mama for a second. She put her index finger to her mouth, and I charged out of the room. Feeling overwhelmed, I went back down, passing Pastor and Dad. Before I went out the door, Dad asked me where I was coming from? Still frightened about what I witnessed, my mind drew a blank."

"This doesn't sound like it will have a good ending."

"My mom came to my rescue and yelled, 'Curtis, you need to remember to flush that toilet.' I knew then, she would always have my back. My dad, in his arrogance, smiled sheepishly. I quickly proceeded outside where I just sat in the grass and didn't say anything for the rest of the day. My emotions were in a high fever!"

"And, you've held this in all of these years?"

"Afraid so. But that rage I was telling you about before. Since that moment, it grew daily, yearly; I mean, I couldn't concentrate on nothing in my life. Kyla, I wanted to take it out on him! I wanted to tell the world, show the world, that Ellis Hickman was a liar and a piece of garbage! My Mama always wanted me to love him. Forgive him. But there's something else that I wanted to do."

"Do what?"

"Kill him!"

Chapter Eight

May 25, 2005

Curtis slept peacefully with Kyla laying her head on his chest and her body on top of his. Slowly, Curtis opens his eyes and turned his head towards the clock on the dresser, that now shows 6:53am.

"Oh Snap!" yelled Curtis, who jumped out of bed, accidentally pushing Kyla to the other side of the bed.

In shock and heart racing, Kyla got up to see what was going on.

Curtis ran into the bathroom. Kyla looked at the clock. "We overslept."

To be on time for his bill collection job, he would need to leave the house no later than 7:05 a.m. Anything after that, there was no guarantee that he would be there by 8:00 a.m. sharp due to the school bus and highway traffic. With him being new at his job, he was still on a ninety-day probation.

With Curtis expressing his feelings last night, he did not bathe as he usually did and had hoped to do so this morning.

"Do you need any help," Kyla asked while getting up from the bed.

"Just lay me some clothes on the bed," Curtis responded.

Kyla went to the closet to see if she could find a shirt that didn't need any ironing. "This orange shirt will have to do."

She quickly grabbed a white tank top, black tie, orange shirt, gray boxer briefs, black socks, and black pants and laid it out on the bed.

Curtis didn't have time to take a shower, so he just washed his face, armpits, and between his legs. He ran out the bathroom naked toward the bed and shivered while grabbing each layer of clothes. He quickly dressed like he was a member of a pit crew.

Curtis looked at the clock, and it was 7:13 a.m.

"Bye, I gotta roll," Curtis said while giving Kyla a quick kiss, who stood by the door to let him out.

Kyla shut the door and went back to bed. Usually, she would be getting ready to head out the door as well, but she asked her manager last week if she could take the day off. She slid in the bed, put the covers on top of her body, and closed her eyes to continue resting.

"Oh my God!" Kyla said while hearing her cell phone ringing.

Her cell phone was on the dresser near the bathroom, and if she needed to answer it or turn it off, it would force her to get out of bed too.

"Screw it; I'll let it go to voicemail," she said to herself.

The phone stopped ringing, and Kyla felt at ease in her position in the bed. Seconds later, the cell phone rang again.

"This better be an emergency," Kyla said out loud while throwing the covers off her body, stomping out of bed, and skipping to her cell phone. She grabbed the phone and noticed it was her best friend April.

"Girl, I hope this is an emergency; if not, you're about to get cursed the hell out," was the first words that came out of Kyla's mouth.

"Cursed out? For what? You should be up anyway, don't you have to get ready to go into work?" asked April.

"Naw, I told you the other day that I had today off."

"Okay, girl, okay, my bad, but hey, you know that I would never call you this time of the morning if it weren't juicy."

"What's up? And hurry up now; I'm ready to go back to bed."

"Go to your TV and turn it to ABC News."

"Huh, why?"

"Don't ask, just do it now, and hurry up before it's too late!"

Kyla moved into the den, dropped down on the couch, picked up the remote control from the coffee table, glanced at the chip wood coffee table, and turned the television on. "What am I supposed to be looking for?"

"Be patient. Give it a second."

Kyla watched the broadcast, and then she saw a familiar face. Her eyebrows arched, her eyes grew big, and her mouth dropped wide." Oh, my God!"

"Do you see what I'm talking about?"

"Hush," Kyla said while trying to hear and stay focused on the news story. She picked up the remote control and turned up the volume. She laid her cell phone on the coffee table and put it on speaker and watched intently. Kyla felt her heart sink into her stomach. "I know that's not my cousin getting arrested, that can't be, not Shawn."

"Yeah, that's him. Hell, I didn't want to believe it myself, but I saw the eleven o'clock news last night, and they were reporting this."

Kyla couldn't believe what she saw. "Students Arrested for a Hazing Death!" She watched her cousin and another young, Black male handcuffed -- heads down trying to avoid the cameras as they were escorted into the county police department.

"I just don't know what to say, I mean, Shawn was the bright Valedictorian from his high school two years ago. I mean, he was supposed to go to medical school, and be the first doctor in our family, and now this mess!" Kyla covered her mouth in disbelief.

"Hey girl, I told it was juicy," April responded.

"Yeah, though I hated for you to call me twice this morning, back to back, I appreciate you for letting me know what's up."

"Twice? Kyla, I only called you once boo-boo," responded April.

"Once?" Kyla picked up her phone, clicked on missed calls. When Kyla saw who called her this morning, she was eager to call them back. "Hey April, let me hit you back."

"Bye!"

Kyla dialed the person that she missed the call.

"Hello!"

"Tasha," said Kyla.

"Hey, Kyla, how are you?" asked Tasha.

"I'm good, your brother and I were just talking about you yesterday."

"I hope it was good!"

"Now, you know, every time your brother talks about you, it's always good! I saw that I missed your call, what's up?"

"Yeah, I didn't mean to disturb you, but I tried calling Curtis a few times this morning, and I didn't reach him. I didn't know if he had paid his bill this time or not," said Tasha.

Kyla laughed. "Yes, his phone bill was paid. I paid it myself, so I know that it is on. Do you have his new number?"

"Oh... Okay, that's good. Yes, he texted it to me about a week ago."

"Well, what I can do is look for his job's number, which I should have saved on my phone, but I got his business card somewhere, and I can text it to you."

"Thank you, Kyla, I would appreciate it."

"No problem. Is there something that I can do to help?"

"Um, naw. I just need to talk to Curtis, but thank you. And by the way, I can't wait for my brother to do the right thing and marry you. You're not just a beautiful woman; you are a beautiful person. I'm glad that he has you in his life."

Kyla smiled. "Oh, my, Tasha, girl. It's too early in the morning to have me crying like this, thank you, thank you, that was so sweet."

"No, thank you, but hey, I gotta go, thank you for your help."

Kyla hung up the phone and was about to get up off the sofa but decided to call Curtis to see if he made it into work on time and safely. While dialing his number, she pondered why he didn't pick up the phone for Tasha? For Evelyn, he would let it go to voice mail and call her back later in a day or two. He would never give his father his number.

While the phone rang, Kyla mysteriously felt a vibration from her seat. She stood up and began pulling the seat cushion off from the couch, where she discovered Curtis' cell phone.

Kyla assumed that the phone slipped down into the couch while he was lying down last night. She grabbed his phone and laid it on the coffee table. While putting the seat cushion back into the couch, Curtis' cell phone started vibrating.

"I'm guessing someone else is trying to get with him, too," Kyla said to herself.

After putting the seat cushions back, Kyla moved toward the kitchen; she glanced down toward his phone and the message, "I miss you," flashed.

Kyla continued to walk to the kitchen with her intuition on high alert. She tried to ignore what she believed she saw and proceeded to fix her a bowl of cereal. Coming back to the den, his phone vibrated again. Curiosity tugged on her as she picked up his phone, and a new message flashed, "Can I see you tonight?"

She dropped the bowl of cereal onto the floor and went forward into looking through Curtis' phone.

"Who the hell wrote this?"

Kyla tried to see who sent the message, but Curtis had his cell phone locked, and she needed to know the six-digit password.

"What could this fool's passcode be? I know it got to be something simple, since he hates remembering new passwords."

Slowly an idea was presented to her. Kyla started thinking of the letters G-L-A-D-Y-S, which equates to the numbers four, five, two, three, nine, and seven.

"Wow, how simple could he have made his password?"

Kyla went into his text messages, and rage emerged from her spirit with each word, his responses, and naked pictures of various females. One particular female Kyla saw, she couldn't quite figure out when she met her, but she was on her knees pleasuring Curtis, who took the picture standing up.

Seconds later, a text came in, "You wouldn't believe what just happened."

***

8:10 a.m.

At the diner, Ellis, Rufus, Carl, and Victor enjoyed their breakfast while listening to Sugar talk about the dating scene.

"Guys these days are sorry as hell! They don't want to work, lounge around all day on the couch, hang out with their boys all night, and then want to come home and expecting their woman to cook as soon as they get home. Shoot, most of my girlfriends are divorced or single because these sorry men," said Sugar.

"One of my cousins told me that she turned gay because guys treated her so bad, she doesn't want anything to do with them," said Carl.

"What! You lying," said Victor.

"Naw, I heard the same thing," said Rufus.

"It's true, I know a few who have experimented on the other side," said Sugar.

"Well, Sugar, if I was your man, they'll think that you are handicap, cause I will carry your fine ass everywhere we go, shoot, your feet wouldn't touch the ground," said Victor.

Sugar and the men at the table started laughing. Victor looked at Sugar with a smile and then blew a kiss at her.

"Hey, let me check on my other tables," Sugar said while laughing.

As always, when Sugar walked away, everyone at the table except for Ellis watched.

"That's a fine piece of a woman," Rufus said while shaking his head and sipping on his cup of coffee.

Ellis noticed Carl looking at his watch.

"You must have to go in today, Carl?" asked Ellis.

"Yes sir, me and another gentleman switched shifts today. So I'm about to leave in a minute. So, what do you have planned today Mr. Ellis?" asked Carl.

Ellis pulled out his new cell phone that Evelyn bought for him for Christmas, laid it on the table, and pulled up his scheduler. "I remember Gladys used to help me out with my scheduler; now I need this to help me remember everything I do. Let me see what I have to do," mentioned Ellis.

While trying to pull up his scheduler, a picture of Tasha popped up on his phone while vibrating the table. Ellis clicked a button on the side of the phone that led her call to voicemail.

"Was that your daughter Tasha?" asked Rufus.

"Yup!" Ellis responded.

"You're not going to answer it?" asked Carl.

"No need! All she is going to do is ask for money, hell she needs to get a job," responded Ellis.

"So Ellis, how often do you talk to your kids," asked Victor.

"I haven't talked to Curtis since the restaurant incident. Tasha will call every other week, which we don't talk long at all. Most of the time, I'm holding the phone in silence. Then as always, she will say 'Dad, can I borrow some money?' Evelyn called me last night and wanted to meet up today at two for lunch," responded Ellis.

"Not trying to tell you what to do, but life is too short. In my line of work, I have seen families wishing they could get another chance, and most of the time they are hurting from things in the past. You need to talk to your kids and try to rectify some issues," said Carl.

Ellis picked up his cup of coffee and started sipping on it. He turned his head toward Carl. "Times like this, I miss

Gladys, she used to be the one to talk to these kids. They say that I don't listen, but if I know what's right, they need to follow my lead."

"But he's right! What we believe is right, they don't see that. I had to learn from my kids. Then assuming they should know, I should have been there to teach them a few things," stated Victor.

"I always expected Gladys to outlive me. Whatever happened at our house, Gladys took care of it," proclaimed Ellis.

"Hey, I got to go, as always, great fellowship," announced Carl while getting up from the table.

"Don't beat no one now," requested Rufus.

"If I do, you'll be the first on the list," responded Carl.

Carl was about to get his bill for breakfast until Ellis intercepted Sugar and insisted on paying for it.

While walking out the door, Carl opened the door for Teresa, who was walking in to pick up a to-go order. While waiting at the bar, she spotted Ellis sitting down with the other men. She gradually walked toward the table.

"Is this seat available," asked Teresa, who slowly walked up to the table with a white mini skirt that showed the imprint of a rubber band size thong.

Ellis' eyes grew big while staring eye-to-eye with Teresa, who for months he had been attempting to avoid her.

"Yes," said Victor, who was caught up in her breast size and voluptuous hips.

Rufus started shaking his head while sipping on his coffee. "As the young folks would say, that's a mighty thirsty brother."

***

9:00 a.m.

Tasha sat on the corner of her bed, staring at the TV, which she put on mute. Wanting to shake off these nerves that she has been fighting for months, she couldn't point a finger on the remedy.

For a moment, Tasha started thinking about Curtis and wishing he could return her call. Growing up, Curtis had always been Tasha's comforter. Evelyn was more concerned about getting family approval.

Without Gladys, Tasha felt like she was drowning, and there was no one around to help her. Gladys' kind spirit, gentle touch, and her love made a difference to Tasha.

The one person who she tried to talk too, hadn't been answering his phone. Even if he did, they never established a rapport, trust, and quality time. That fairy tale of having a father-daughter relationship was good for the cartoons. It was hard to have a general conversation with dear ole dad. How could she explain what she's going through?

When life felt like a tight rope, Tasha remembered her father saying that therapy was ridiculous, Black folks don't get therapy, and it's a waste of money. Even when Gladys gave a great thesis of why her baby needs to get the help, Ellis would always say we can pray about it, or she can just take a whooping.

Tasha got up, walked to her dresser, and pulled out her mother's obituary. Tears fell down her face.

"I wish you weren't gone, Mama, I miss you," stated Tasha.

She laid back on her bed, thinking of what's her purpose in life. No support from her father, no love from her sister, no communication from her brother, and no friends that she could count on was on her mind.

She went back into her drawer and pulled out a Wavery knife that she got from the kitchen. She looked at her arms and saw the many scars that she started but did not go deep enough because of fear of pain.

Tasha laid the Wavery knife on the bed and thought about taking some medicine to end her pain. She went into her medicine cabinet and only had one bottle of Aspirin that was expired about a year ago. Knowing that her roommate Renee was at the library, she went into her room and stole several over-the-counter medicines. She also discovered a couple of prescription medicines that she took from the cabinet.

After grabbing the medicines, she went into the living room, pulled out some printing paper from the printer, wrote a message, and then walked out toward the living room.

Tasha consumed all the medicines while laying back on the couch, hoping that she won't feel any pain; hoping that this would ease all of her life's problems.

"I'm coming to see you, Mama!"

***

11:15 a.m.

Curtis walked into the bathroom, stood in front of the mirror, turned on the faucet, and started throwing water in his face. He closed his eyes and yelled, "Can I just get a break?"

His coworker Ben looked at him and smiled while he washed his hands.

"Sounds like you're having fun?"

"Dude, these people and their threats. They know they owe a bill, just pay it! I shouldn't be taking all these curse-outs."

"Hey, that's the life of a bill collector. If they didn't screw up, then we wouldn't have jobs."

"Yeah, I guess you're right, but dang."

When Ben walked out the door, Tim Beasley, better known as Beasley, and the man who helped Curtis get his job at this collection agency, walked into the bathroom.

"What's up Ben?" said Beasley while giving him a fist pump.

"Hey, it looks like your boy can't hang," Ben said with a grin on his face.

"Can't hang?" Curtis said while standing straight up from the sink.

Curtis looked at Ben up and down with a lion's intimidating stare.

Ben smiled, gave the peace sign with his left hand, and walked out the bathroom.

"What's up homie? I hope what he was saying ain't true," said Beasley while walking up on Curtis.

Curtis leaned back over to the sink to splash water in his

face.

Seconds later, he stood back up, grabbed a paper towel to wipe his face. Once he finished wiping, he kept noticing Beasley staring at him. He wanted to ignore it, but that nagging feeling inside wouldn't allow him to let it go.

"Dude, why the hell are you staring? Do you like what you see or something?" responded Curtis.

Beasley stepped back and kept staring at him.

"Hey, I'm not going to quit... If you want that referral money, I know I got to stay these freakin ninety days," said Curtis.

Beasley started shaking his head, then turned around and walked up in the stall.

Curtis waited until Beasley finished peeing until he spoke to him.

Once done, Beasley looked at Curtis and started shaking his head while washing his hands.

"Man, what's really wrong? Talk to me! You were the top collector at your last job 'til they sold that portfolio overseas. Yo, I got a feeling that what's really wrong with you doesn't involve the job. It's something more, probably something I've been warning you, and now it's biting you on the ass," said Beasley.

Curtis just stood there, with nothing to say.

"Cat got your tongue?" Beasley sarcastically stated.

Curtis looked over Beasley, and it was like he was

reading his life story all over his head.

Beasley then walked around the other stalls, making sure no one else was there and then came back toward Curtis. "Hey, you got my text?"

Curtis normally puts his phone in his right pocket, but once he realized that there was no phone, he started going in all of his pockets, even patting himself down. "I don't know where I put my phone."

Beasley walked up to Curtis. He was so close that Curtis could smell Beasley's Polo cologne.

In a whisper, "Are you still…"

"What's up fellas," yelled Big Hurt, who walked into a stall.

Big Hurt, as he is known at the job, but his real name was Jim Jackson, stood 6'10', 280 pounds of muscle, and gold teeth was part of the security team at the job.

Curtis and Beasley looked at each other.

Looking at Curtis's expression, Big Hurt answered Beasley's question. "Uhhhhhhhhhh," screamed Big Hurt at the stall.

"Are you pissing a water fountain," asked Beasley.

"Shiiii… feels like it," Big Hurt said while flushing the toilet.

Big Hurt walked toward the faucet. Beasley and Curtis moved to the side so he can have some room.

"Once again, congrats on your engagement," said

Beasley.

"Engagement?" repeated Curtis.

"Yeah, what are you surprised or something?" asked Big Hurt.

Before Curtis could have replied, Beasley jumped in. "I haven't told him yet."

"Oh, Okay," responded Big Hurt while washing his hands.

"Again, congrats to you and now your fiancé Naomi," stated Beasley.

"Appreciate cha," Big Hurt responded with a smile on his face.

"So, how did you propose? Were you romantic or smooth with it?" asked Curtis, who was being curious.

"Man, on the real, for quite a while my girl been acting funny. Originally, I thought she was messing around or doing some messed up illegal stuff behind my back. But I had to think, we been together for eight years, the last couple of weddings she's been the bridesmaid, and she probably ready to marry this ninja. So, I saved up money at this job and my security job on the weekend at the club, went to the jewelry store, and before she walked out the door this morning, I got down on both knees and popped the question, and the rest was history," said Big Hurt.

Curtis started nodding his head, and once Big Hurt finished wiping his hands, Curtis gave him dap.

"So, when you become married, are you still going to

have those get togethers at your crib, like the one I took my boy Curtis and his girl last year?" asked Beasley.

Big Hurt started looking at his watch while walking toward the door.

"Hey, you know it, marriage ain't going to change me playa, but hey, I holla at you fellas later on," said Big Hurt.

Once Big Hurt walked out the door, Curtis and Beasley just stared at each other for the moment. Beasley started walking backward toward the door.

"Engaged!" announced Beasley, "You heard him, right?"

Realizing that his fifteen-minute break was turning into thirty minutes, Curtis started walking toward the door. Curtis snuck back into his cubicle, trying to avoid his manager, and having to explain why he was late coming back from break.

Soon as he sat down, his desk phone rang and noticed it was the front lobby calling him. He answered the phone and was asked to pick up an item in the front lobby. Curtis got up, told his co-worker Janet, whose cube was right next to him, that they called him up to the front lobby.

Curtis walked into the front lobby, and before he could walk up to the receptionist desk, Kyla, who seemed to have come out of nowhere, immediately greeted him. "Hey, sweetie, how are you?"

"I'm straight, a little tired, but I'll manage, so what brings you here?"

"Well, something came up as soon as you left, so I called you, but you didn't answer. So I kinda stumbled onto your phone when I was watching television," Kyla stated while pulling out his cell phone from her purse.

"Thank you, baby. I was rushing this morning, and I totally forgot it. So, what came up this morning after I left?" asked Curtis.

Kyla shoved his cell phone in his face!

"This fool!" responded Kyla.

Curtis tried to grab his phone, but Kyla kept moving her arms, antagonizing him.

"Hey, stop it, I'm at my job!" yelled Curtis.

"Screw you Curtis, like you screwing this whore!" responded Kyla.

Kyla attempted to slap Curtis until he caught her wrist in the air. Scared of the situation, the receptionist called security.

"Hey, you don't have to do this," said Curtis.

Kyla kicked Curtis in the ankle, and he quickly let go of his grip. Curtis started to create a fist, but immediately noticed the cameras around the lobby area and decided to move a few steps before he did something that he really would regret.

"Just give me my phone and leave," Curtis said in a calm demeanor but sweating like he just got finished washing his head.

"Why? Why? I was there for you Curtis, and this is how you treat me."

"When I get off from work, we'll talk," responded Curtis.

"Naw, cause when I wanted to talk, you had other things to do, or refused to let me know what's going on in your life. And I thought what we had was special. You actually opened up your heart to me last night. But you were only using me while you entertain all types of females and using my dang phone that I got for your broke self," Kyla stated while pointing at the black bag.

"What's in the bag?" asked Curtis while pointing at it.

"Well, my dear Curtis, this is all of your stuff. I cleared your belongings out of my house."

Kyla grabbed the bag and dumped it all over the lobby floor.

Curtis was pissed to see some of his clothes were cut up or written on.

"Well, you may be wondering where are your other clothes. Well, most of your stuff, I bought! To release some stress, I cut up quite a few. Especially your expensive pairs of shoes, but hey, since you love to creep, that other female can buy you some more shoes. Since I was tired of ripping some of your clothes, I drove by the Lincoln Bridge, where most of the homeless congregate, and I gave them some of your stuff. And so you wouldn't think I was too much of a devil, here is a bag full of all the clothes you have remaining," said Kyla.

"KYLA! You going to make me kill you," said Curtis, who was charging up to her until he saw in the corner of his eye Big Hurt and another security guard coming into the lobby to diffuse the situation.

Before Big Hurt could say a word, "I'm okay, we are okay!" responded Curtis, who never took his eyes off of Kyla, hoping he would just walk away.

"Wait, wait a minute, I know you!" yelled Kyla.

***

2:00 p.m.

Ellis walked in the mortuary and was greeted by Allatoona Beverly, who was the same age as Gladys, and had worked for Ellis for twenty-seven years as the secretary.

"Hey, Ellis," Mrs. Beverly said while walking up to Ellis.

Ellis, with a smile on his face, walked up and hugged Mrs. Beverly.

Mrs. Beverly was the type of woman anyone would love to hire, and families loved her. She was warm, kind, sweet, honest, held no punches, and she could make a peach cobbler that was so good, it made you want to do the splits.

"Mrs. Beverly, tell me something good," Ellis said.

"Well, I'm blessed to see another day, and I'm about to be a great-grandma."

"A great-grandma?" Ellis said with a shocked look on his face.

"Yeah, my eighteen-year-old granddaughter is about to have a little girl," Mrs. Beverly voiced.

"Now you got me feeling old. I remember when all of your kids were born." Ellis twisted his lips.

"Yeah, they're grown now. So, as long as they take care

of themselves, I'm good. I'm done raising kids," Mrs. Beverly said, wiping her forehead as she took a deep breath.

"I hear ya. Speaking of daughters, is Evelyn in her office?" Ellis asked.

"No, she's in the conference room with the Brook's family. They lost their son in a motorcycle accident last night."

"Ok, well, I'll just walk around for a minute and may go speak to everyone in the embalming room. If she comes out anytime soon, just let her know that I am here, please." Ellis strolled away.

Mrs. Beverly nodded her head.

Ellis walked a few steps, and then stopped. He turned around and went back to Mrs. Beverly. "Mrs. Beverly, can I ask you something?"

"Sure, if it's money, well, I need to ask my employer for a raise," said Mrs. Beverly.

Ellis chuckled.

Mrs. Beverly smiled and then sat down in a chair, and Ellis sat right beside her. "How did you handle the pain and grief when your husband Charles Lee, died," asked Ellis.

"One day at a time, Ellis, one day at a time."

"I never expected to be in this situation. Each day gets harder and harder."

"Well, life is not fair. There are just certain things that you cannot control, and you must accept it. I didn't expect to be a widow for almost nine years now. Charles and I had plans, but that's how life is. Yes, I miss him, but like Gladys, their time here is over, and they are in a better place."

Ellis nodded his head while he clenched his hands on his lap.

"What you need to do now is be the best father for your kids because you are all they got," recommended Mrs. Beverly.

Ellis shook his head, "It's too late for me."

"It's only too late when you don't want to put the effort out there. Or, if you're dead!"

Before Ellis could respond, the conference room door opened and Evelyn escorted the family to the door.

Ellis quickly rose and then turned toward Mrs. Beverly. "I miss Oh Charles, he had so much energy and was very vibrant. I was saddened that he fell ill and died."

"Yeah, same here," said Mrs. Beverly.

Once the family left, Evelyn walked up to her father, gave him a hug, and asked for fifteen minutes so she can take care of a little paperwork.

Evelyn walked into her office, sat down, and a few seconds later, an anonymous phone number call rang on her cell phone, which was on her desk. She started not to answer it but changed her mind. "Hello," answered Evelyn.

"You have a collect call from Curtis Hickman in Metro Jail Station. If you want to accept, press one on your phone."

Evelyn, as her hands trembled, quickly pressed one.

"Hey, Evelyn, I need help. I'm in jail!"

"What!" responded Evelyn.

"Yeah, it's a long story, but I need your help to get me out of here!"

"Why are you calling me? Why not any of your friends?"

"Are you going to get me out or not?"

With anger in her heart, Evelyn was about to hang up the phone and let Curtis stay in jail until she glanced at a picture of her mother on her desk. Remembering that her mother always preached about family and taking care of each other.

"I'll see what I can do," responded Evelyn.

"Thanks, and please don't tell your father."

"He's our father!" responded Evelyn before she hung up the phone.

Chapter Nine

Since her mother's passing, Evelyn leaned on Mrs. Beverly as a shield and role model of wisdom. Throughout the issues with her family, Mrs. Beverly has not only prayed with her but also gave her a listening ear when she needed to scream.

When the Brooks family arrived at the funeral home to discuss funeral arrangements for their son who was killed in a motorcycle accident, with each mourning family, Mrs. Beverly greeted them, gave her condolences, asked them to have a seat in the lounge area, and headed to Evelyn's office to inform her that the next clients had arrived.

Today, when Mrs. Beverly knocked on the door, there was an unusual presence. Typically Mrs. Beverly knocked once. This time, Mrs. Beverly knocked multiple times until Evelyn informed her to come in. Mrs. Beverly walked in, and it was apparent that Evelyn had lost her gleeful spirit.

Evelyn's body was there, but her mind was temporarily in another area code. Besides her holding her head down, there was a box a Kleenex beside her, the picture frame faced down, and papers scattered all around her desk like a tropical storm came through.

"Hey, Evelyn, your next appointment is here," Mrs. Beverly reminded her.

"Um, okay," Evelyn reluctantly replied.

Mrs. Beverly walked up to Evelyn until she finally

realized that Mrs. Beverly stood right in front of her. It was evident that something had her in a chokehold. Evelyn didn't change her facial expression; instead, she gave out a loud sigh, sat back in her chair, and turned her neck casting her eyes at Mrs. Beverly. Wiping her face with the palm of her hand, she fought to keep her tears from falling. "Mrs. Beverly, I just don't understand, I just don't."

Before Mrs. Beverly could say a word, she stepped back and handed her a couple of tissues. "Talk to me."

On top of trying to run a funeral home business and dealing with her family, Evelyn felt that she couldn't afford to deal with any more strains.

Evelyn grabbed the photo and pulled it up toward her face, then immediately slapped it down back on the desk. "For years I had his back, I gave him some time thinking he is trying to get himself together, but I just had a feeling, that, that I was wasting my time. Yesterday makes nine years of being with Troy, and when I asked him, where are we going, he just stood there, with nothing to say."

Mrs. Beverly rubbed Evelyn's back. She knew how special Troy was to her and hoped that he would finally step up and make a commitment. "Evelyn sweetie, you may not want to hear this, but I got to let you know, this may be a good move for the both of you."

Evelyn looked up with a puzzled expression on her face?

"Evelyn, you are a beautiful woman with a lot of great things to offer any man! You are a beautiful, talented, educated, and a God-fearing woman. For nine years, you gave him the best of you, and if he cannot see this now, then he is either blind or ignorant. This could be the test that you need to see what direction you need to make for yourself. Seems like you know the answer."

Evelyn smiled; her tears soon cleared.

"You always have the right words to say regardless if it feels good or stings. I know I needed to hear that, thank you," stated Evelyn, who stood and embraced Mrs. Beverly.

"Thank you, sweetie, but take it from me, I saw it quite often in my lifetime, women chasing men. Hell, men chasing women. If they really want to be with you, they'd stop running."

After she embraced Mrs. Beverly, remembering that she had a family waiting on her, she pulled out her drawer keys, found the one to her desk, opened up the cabinet drawer on the bottom of her desk, opened her purse, pulled out her mini mirror and wiped her face.

"Hey, your face is good. I'll straighten out all of these documents and put it back in the cabinet," acknowledged Mrs. Beverly.

"Thank you," said Evelyn, who pulled out the cabinet keys from her pocket, handed to Mrs. Beverly and then rushed out so she wouldn't keep the Brooks family waiting any longer.

Mrs. Beverly put all the documents in the cabinet. Evelyn left her purse in her chair, and Mrs. Beverly noticed a stack of papers on the bottom of the drawer.

"What a pretty purse, but I be crazy if I pay this amount for this," she said to herself while picking it up.

She went to put the purse back in the drawer, but something caught her attention. She picked up the documents and began reading.

***

2:50 p.m.

Evelyn chose a local Chinese restaurant for lunch. Ellis didn't care for Chinese food, but since he gave her the liberty to choose any restaurant she wanted to go, he didn't debate her decision.

For about twenty minutes, Evelyn spoke about the business and how many funerals they were planning to serve in the next two weeks. As usual, Ellis always enjoyed listening about his business, but a strange feeling popped him in his face, and he felt like he had a new purpose. Looking at Evelyn, for the first time in his life, his eyes began to see something within her. "Evelyn, you look like your mother. Those eyes, her cheeks, and the way you talk. That is spot on of Gladys."

Memories of a young, adorable Evelyn formed of her hugging his leg and begging for him to stay at home instead of leaving.

Evelyn didn't realize how bad he wanted to be with her, but bills had to be paid.

Then he thought of how many other moments he missed. Gladys' message of "I need to spend time with my kids" slapped him in the face that second.

Thoughts of Gladys formulated throughout Ellis' mind until he couldn't hear Evelyn. Ellis smiled, and Evelyn assumed that he liked what she was saying.

Ellis saw a young couple who were walking to their seats. They looked to be in their mid-twenties. The young lady held a rose and the young man walked up to the table, grabbed, and pulled out her chair for her. Assuming that this was their first date, Ellis laughed to himself, thinking that the chivalry stuff won't last too long.

"You alright, Daddy?" Evelyn asked.

"Yeah, I was just thinking of your mama and how that couple reminds me of her and me," Ellis responded.

"Dad, could you, or would you mind stop talking about mama. I mean, it seems like every five seconds there's a mama story," Evelyn requested.

"I'll try, but it's hard. I miss that woman every day. One day, when you and Troy finally get married, you would understand."

With no response, Ellis thought it was quite odd, because she loves defending him.

Evelyn regularly talked about the funeral business because usually, hearing about making money or things we do in the community made him happy. The thoughts of her brother were crossing her mind. *What did he do? Why did he do it? Why can't he just freaking grow up?* Thinking of Tasha, *Why hasn't she called? Why haven't I heard from her lately?*

For the moment, both of them ate in silence. Ellis snapped out of his trance and realized that Evelyn had stopped talking. Evelyn looked at her watch hoping that they can finish soon so she could bail her brother out of jail.

Ellis noticed Evelyn's mannerisms and wondered what was on her mind. "So, have you heard from your siblings?" asked Ellis.

"I talked to Curtis a little bit today, and it's been a while since I spoke with Tasha."

Evelyn didn't want to mention that Curtis was in jail because he would add it to his long list of disappointments of his son; that alone would be a thirty-minute conversation about his failures.

"And you, when have you heard from your other kids?"

"Well, one is here with me now, whom I enjoy spending some quality time with. So I'm not totally a failure with my kids." Ellis smiled. "One called this morning, but I didn't answer, and the other one, well, maybe one day we'll get back in to good terms."

"Don't say that you're a failure dad. Trust me, I know a few people who wish they had a dad like you," said Evelyn.

"Thank you, baby, your mama always said I should have spent more time with you kids, but my goal was to see you kids not to struggle like I did, with a single mother, and a father who had multiple relationships with every woman across town," responded Ellis.

Evelyn smiled and hoped that he wasn't going to mention their mother, but knowing her father, that would have been impossible. It would be like telling a crackhead to not smoke crack that was in his hand. "So, why didn't you answer the phone when Tasha called, heck I'm wondering when she would return my call."

"Every time she calls, we really don't talk. For minutes I just hold the phone up in silence. Then she may ask for money, and that's it! If that's all we are going to do, then I can just save my money and time," responded Ellis.

Evelyn just listened, continuing to eat her food, and she didn't say a word back. That moment, the thoughts of Troy were raining down on her. Even though Mrs. Beverly was right, Evelyn never loved a man more than him.

"Hopefully, soon, we can all see eye to eye, Daddy."

"Perhaps, but it would actually take God being a mediator for me and Curtis to get along."

"Well Dad, you can't put all the blame on him. I mean you weren't the Father of the Year material."

"So, I was a failure, is that what you are saying?"

Evelyn shook her head and grabbed her cup of water. "No, you want me to say that to validate your statement so we can feel bad for you! A lot of things happening, you put on yourself. I mean, you pushed mama, and Curtis saw it. How do you think he feels seeing this?"

"Yeah, I did do that. And yes, I'm haunted by that scar every day…" Ellis stopped in mid-sentence.

Evelyn looked on, quickly glancing at her watch.

"But, I'm about to share with you something that I need you not to repeat to anyone, okay?" whispered Ellis.

Evelyn nodded her head. "Yeah, Daddy?"

"I had the feeling that your mama was messing around. I found a few things, saw some things that didn't add up, and when I confronted her, I was pissed and laid hands on her."

Evelyn acted surprised. Knowing what she found, she tried to keep cool. "Are you sure, what did you find?"

Ellis looked up and saw a big group walking into the restaurant. He noticed in the corner of his eye, the hosts bringing together several tables and chairs. In the middle of the group was a senior couple. The lady used a cane to help her balance, and the man followed behind her.

"How do you like this Grandma," one of the kids said while holding a large cake that read, "Happy Anniversary."

Ellis stared at the older couple and their family celebrating their anniversary and wondered how life would be if Gladys were still alive.

Evelyn watched her father staring at the other family and declined to ask about what other evidence he discovered.

"That should've been your mother and me," said Ellis.

Peeking at her watch, Evelyn was mute.

"You must got something to take care of?"

"Somewhat," she responded.

"Oh, you and Troy, huh?"

"No. Troy and I are taking a little break," Evelyn said, then suddenly regretted mentioning it.

"A break? You guys been together for some years. I thought he would finally get his self together to marry you," responded Ellis.

"Let it go!"

The waitress came by, and Ellis asked for the bill. He turned his head toward Evelyn and shook it. "See, I hope you now see why I wanted you to get an abortion. I knew that he wasn't any good."

Evelyn's eyes opened wide, and she dropped her fork onto the floor. A hint of rage slowly lit. She glared at her father for a second, and then she turned her head.

"Your mama wanted to keep the baby. You were about fifteen. We had to raise another child. Hell, I knew she was mad at me for a while, but I know that was the best decision."

"It's about time to go Dad," responded Evelyn who wanted to avoid the conversation.

Ellis smiled. "You know it was to be true, the best decision, you wasn't ready to become a mother."

Evelyn grabbed her purse and looked toward her father with tears streaming down.

"Best decision? Yeah, I got pregnant young. Yes, I made a mistake. Each day I wonder what type of mother I would be. I wanted to keep the baby. You sit here like you're Jesus Christ, who never made a mistake or never had anyone to help you when you messed up."

"Calm down. You're making a scene."

"And do you remember when you told me when you found out I was pregnant? You said I was being a slut, you said I was stupid, you said that you would be embarrassed to go to church with me because you would feel like a hypocrite. So I ask you, Daddy… was it the best decision for you? I mean… I understand that you have your perfect image! Because you surely didn't care about me then."

The waiter came by the table with the bill in his hand. Evelyn dropped forty dollars on the table. "Keep the change."

Evelyn rose glaring at her father. "Bye Daddy!" Evelyn

stormed toward the door.

Ellis sat there, with his arms crossed, staring at the door, replaying the last thirty seconds in his head, and what could he have said. He finally got up and walked out the door, hoping he could catch up with Evelyn to make things right. Ellis saw Evelyn getting into her car.

"Evelyn! Evelyn!" yelled Ellis.

Evelyn saw her father while turning on the ignition. Shaking her head and debating her next move, she opened the door and got out of her car.

Ellis met Evelyn in front of it. "Evelyn…"

"…Wait! No need to say anything, plus I don't have time for it now! Take care, Daddy," Evelyn said while embracing her father.

"You too, maybe we can do this again," Ellis replied, hoping she would say yes.

Evelyn smiled and proceeded to get in her car. Ellis followed behind her. Once Evelyn was in her car, Ellis shut her door and strode to his truck.

By the time Ellis got to his truck, he saw Evelyn had pulled out the restaurant driveway. He opened up his truck door, got inside, put the key in the ignition, and sat there wondering when it comes to his family, why was he such a failure.

Suddenly a buzzing noise was coming out of nowhere. Thinking that a bee had flown into his truck, he jumped all around like he was performing the electric slide, and then he remembered that he left his cell phone in the middle console. The voice mail sign popped on. He noticed that he missed eight calls from Carl, which was strange since he knew he was patrolling, making sure our community was safe.

***

4:10 p.m.

Evelyn walked up the steps to the police station. She saw Kyla walking with another female toward her. "Hey, Kyla, what happened to my brother?"

Kyla stormed right past her like she was never there. Evelyn kept moving because she was in immediate need of answers. Once she posted bail, she waited about fifteen minutes until the officer brought Curtis to the counter. Evelyn was disappointed in seeing her brother being led out like he was a child, but what stood out was his enormous swollen lip and black eye.

"What the hell happened?" Evelyn yelled, "Did they do this?"

"Yo, let's get the hell out of here," Curtis responded.

Evelyn didn't respond. Once he finished signing several release documents, both of them quickly paced to Evelyn's SUV. Once they both were inside it, Evelyn demanded answers.

"Look, I'm having a bad day. You better tell me the truth. What in hell happened? What in God's name did you do?" She slammed her fist onto the steering wheel.

Curtis tilted his head to the side, ran his fingers through his hair. "Kyla saw messages on my cell phone from another women. There were pictures too. Naked pictures. She came to my work and confronted me making a huge scene. I kept my cool trying to calm her down. She wanted to know who it was.

The desk clerk called security. So when security was escorting her out, I tried to get my phone. Instead of handing it to me, she pulled out my cell phone and showed security the pictures. Well... the naked lady in the picture was one of the security guards fiancé."

"What?? You joking right?"

Shaking his head. "We call him Big Hurt. So once he saw the pictures from my phone, he snapped and came charging towards me. That's when the clerk called the cops."

"Wait, let me get this straight," said Evelyn staring at her brother. "You left your cell phone at her spot, not your spot, because really you are homeless."

Curtis was about to comment until Evelyn put her index finger in the air to indicate to Curtis to shut the hell up!

Feeling embarrassed that she had to get him out of jail, he leaned back toward the passenger side window.

"Your girlfriend finds your phone with a nasty message and picture from your side broad. Girlfriend gets pissed, which I couldn't blame her. So, she decides to confront you at the job. Knowing that you depend on her for your living arrangements. You didn't want any trouble and tried to calm things down. Again, she was pissed and hurt. But in reality, you didn't want another person to find out. She puts your business out there. Security see's the picture. And Big Hurt...that's what you call him, punched you in the face."

"Yeah."

"Wow Curtis. You broke up your home and someone else's home. Looking at your face, you took a good beat down. Wait... I'm guessing you got fired and no place to stay. You're some kind of stupid."

Curtis laid his seat back. "Just drive!"

Evelyn shook her head in disappointment. "When Curtis? When are you going to get your life together? You're more than worthless. I should've let you rot in that cell. At least, you'd have a roof over your head."

Curtis sat in silence, listening to Evelyn, and he couldn't deny that she was preaching the truth to him.

Evelyn turned on the ignition, and then her cell phone rang. She picked it up and saw that it was her father. A funny feeling started tingling all over her. She didn't know if it was how she spoke to her father or how bad she held in the pain that she felt about him.

"Hey Daddy… What!... Oh my God!... Where?... I'm on the way!"

"What's going on?" asked Curtis sitting straight up from his seat.

"Tasha was just rushed to the hospital! She tried to kill herself!"

Chapter Ten

Ellis sat in the chair, trembling right beside his daughter. He got up and paced around the room to knock out his fears, but it didn't help. In his mind, he heard Gladys.

You need to spend time with her. She wants to spend time with her daddy! Maybe we can help her with a doctor.

The words of Gladys kept resonating like she was a ghost standing right beside him.

Ellis sat back down and moved the chair next to his daughter's bed. "God, please give her strength. Don't let her die."

The doctor was in the room about ten minutes ago and informed him that they were able to pump all of those drugs out of her system, and she should be fine.

For years, Tasha craved her father's attention and the guilt of not being there when she wanted him dug deep inside him.

Ellis walked toward the window and glanced at the puffy clouds and light blue sky. "Lord, I asked you why? Why did you have to take my wife? Why? I got too much on my plate, I mean I got faith in you, but I feel like I'm in the middle of the highway, and I see two cars coming from both sides, and I can't move, and I need you, I…"

Ellis turned around and stared at Tasha. "Why, Tasha?

Why would you want to cut your days short?"

He turned his head back toward the window and looked into the sky.

It wasn't her fault! Maybe I was to blame! I should have listened to you Gladys. I should have listened to you!

A small tap came from the door. Ellis jumped, and then turned around. He signaled Carl to come in.

"Thank you," Ellis stated while reaching out to hug Carl.

"Hey, no need to thank me, no need."

Carl looked toward Tasha lying in the bed asleep.

"How is she doing, Ellis?"

"The doctors said that she will be alright, they had to pump out all of those drugs she took, she should be good," responded Ellis, who was still in shock of the circumstance.

"So, what about you, how are you doing?"

"Truthfully, I can't even answer that," Ellis said while sitting back down in the chair.

Carl put his hand on Ellis' shoulder and gradually massaged his shoulder. He tried to think of words of affirmation that could bring some type of joy, but nothing came.

"Carl, I can't, I just can't take another hit like this. One more hit, and I'm going to open up one of our coffins, and just lay in it because it's clearly time for me to go."

"Don't say that Mr. Hickman; we all go through different challenges in life."

"Life must really hate me," said Ellis.

"That's bull!" blurted Victor, who was standing by the door eavesdropping, waiting on the perfect opportunity to come in.

Carl shook Victor's hand, and Ellis was about to get up from his seat until Victor instructed him to remain seated. "I hope you didn't mind. I told the whole breakfast crew," said Victor.

"I appreciate it, but you didn't have too," replied Ellis.

"Nonsense, we're like another family to you. I'll be pissed off if something happened to you, and I didn't know nothing about it," stated Victor.

Neither Ellis nor Carl said a word. Victor walked up to the bed.

"Where's your other two," Victor said.

Like a rabbit leaping from a hat, Evelyn and Curtis popped in the room.

"I guess that answered your question," said Ellis while getting up from his seat.

Evelyn ran to her father and embraced him. "Why?" she screamed out.

Ellis rubbed her back. "She's still here with us, and everything will be okay."

Curtis black eye and swollen lip were as clear as light in a dark closet.

"Dang, that boy took a whoopin " Victor whispered to

Carl.

Without hesitation, Carl nodded.

Evelyn let her father go, walked up to Tasha, grabbed her hand, and rubbed it with her thumb.

"Hey," said Curtis.

"Hey," replied Ellis.

"Boy, go and hug your father," Victor demanded.

Curtis turned around and gave Victor an ice-cold look, and was about to comment, but saw Carl in his police uniform and choose to keep his mouth closed and walked to the other side of the bed.

Carl approached Ellis. "I just wanted to drop by and give you support. I'll check back with you later tonight."

"Oh, can you wait for a second?" Ellis asked.

"Evelyn and Curtis, these are my friends Victor and Carl. These gentlemen and some other guys go and eat breakfast during the week. But I wanted to let you know before he goes, that Officer Carl here is the one that saved your sister."

"I told you, Mr. Hickman, you don't have to give me credit," responded Carl.

"Yes, I Do!"

"What happened?" Curtis asked.

"Well," said Carl, who was the center of attention with his heroic deed. "I was visiting my niece. I didn't know they stayed at the same apartment complex, and I was going upstairs, and I heard a lady screaming. It sounded like it was coming from downstairs. Once I heard that, I ran downstairs, and I saw a door wide open, and I saw her roommate, I think, Renee."

"It's Renee," Evelyn answered.

"Well, I had seen Renee standing over Tasha. She stated Tasha had taken some pills. I asked Renee to call 9-1-1. Seconds later, the EMT came over. While I was at the apartment, I saw her picture from her cell phone and your family picture in her room. Which led me to call you, Mr. Hickman."

"Again, thank you!" replied Ellis, who wiped his tears.

Evelyn walked up to Carl and gave him a strong bear hug that had him asking her to loosen up her grip. She grabbed his head and pushed it forward, and then she kissed him on the cheek, which left an imprint like it was a fossil.

"I'm not going to kiss you, but I will give you a hug, there is such a thing as a good cop," said Curtis.

Curtis shook Carl's hand and then embraced him with the other arm around his back.

"Where is Renee?" asked Evelyn.

"I believe she said she was going to her mother's house. She was quite shaken up. I asked was she coming to the hospital, and she replied no. She stated that hospitals make her nervous," replied Carl.

"Okay, I believe I have her number, I'll let her know that she's ok," said Evelyn.

"Please do," mentioned Ellis.

Victor walked toward Ellis and laid his hand on his shoulder. "Hey, let's get some fresh air," requested Victor.

Not feeling like arguing, Ellis nodded his head. "I'm going to be downstairs for a minute."

While walking toward the elevator, Carl reminded Ellis that if he needed anything, to please contact him. Victor kept his emotions in check, but all through his mind, he wanted to hold his friend and not let him go. It's not only tough to lose a wife, but having to deal with issues with your family, maintain a business, and someone close to you wanting to attempt to take their life away put a toll on anyone. Victor wondered if he was a strong enough man to handle this stress.

Ellis, Carl, and Victor walked up to the elevator. Ellis attempted to touch the button on the elevator door to open it, but suddenly his fingers started to shake uncontrollably, and then the rest of his body followed.

Ellis' knees started to buckle; Victor caught him before he fell.

Ellis screamed in deep-boned agony.

The strain and stress of Tasha's attempted suicide and family issues were breaking his soul apart.

Victor and Carl both simultaneously hugged Ellis from each shoulder letting him know that it was okay to cry out.

Head down, hands over his eyes, *Men don't cry*, Ellis was thinking.

Carl pulled one of his handkerchiefs out of his pocket and gave it to Ellis.

The elevator door opened, and before they stepped in, Rufus, Dean, and Pastor Houston were inside, waiting to walk out.

Chapter Eleven

Evelyn sat down in the chair next to Tasha's bed, took her high heels off, which she was relieved to let her feet stretch. "Thank you, Jesus" she said silently to herself. She went into her purse, pulled out her flats, rubbed her feet, and slipped them on.

Curtis kept staring at Tasha, still mortified by the scars she left on her arms. Since they were little, Curtis made a vow to always watch over his little sister.

"You might as well sit down Curtis and let her rest a little bit," Evelyn suggested.

For years Cutis kept his sister close to him. Throughout the years, he knew in his heart that his sister secretly suffered from depression. For years, their mother wanted to get her help, but their father didn't believe in therapy and thought it was a waste of money and time.

"I would have done anything that she asked me too," Curtis said who stopped watching Tasha and walked toward the window that highlighted the city in the background. The day was settling down, and the night was about to make its debut. He looked around and watched Evelyn close her eyes as she prayed. He hoped that she could say a prayer for him. With the emotions and hassle of the day, Curtis felt the need to walk off his tension.

"Hey, I'm about to step out for a second," Curtis stated while walking out. He decided to walk into the bathroom to fully checkout his war wound. *I should have bobbed and weaved.*

While leaving the bathroom, his stomach growled, and he saw the sign to the vending machine area. Once he got to the vending machine, he tried to find eighty-five cents on him, but nothing was in his pockets but his license, two pennies, and lent.

Curtis laid his forehead on the vending machine and punched it until his knuckles became numb.

"If you expect something to fall out, you're not hitting it hard enough," a familiar voice sounded off.

Curtis turned around, and Pastor Houston held six one-dollar bills in his hand. "Here you go, Curtis."

"Hey, I can't take your money," expressed Curtis, who desired those potato chips in section E6.

"You remind me so much of your father," Pastor Houston said, smiling while approaching the vending machine. "I was thinking about getting some chips."

Pastor Houston bought three bags of chips and two sodas.

"Here you go, Curtis," Pastor insisted while handing him two bags of chips and a soda.

"Thank you, Pastor!"

"No problem, but don't let your pride cause you to miss out on your blessings now," explained Pastor Houston.

Curtis nodded his head and pretended that he agreed with him because he was so thankful his stomach stopped doing flips.

"While you're at the hospital, you may want to get an ice pack on your face," suggested Pastor Houston.

"I'll be okay, Pastor. I've been in a few scraps back in the days, it will heal," noted Curtis.

Pastor smiled. "Okay, well before I got saved, I used to box. I was pretty good, never professionally, just an amateur, but life happens, my girlfriend at the time told me she was pregnant, and my attentions were to provide a steady income to take care of them."

"Ever thought about getting back into it?" Curtis asked.

"At one point, I did, but God had another responsibility for me," replied Pastor Houston.

While walking down the hallway, they came to the waiting area.

"Hey, do you mind if I asked you something?"

Curtis was skeptical at first but agreed. The simple fact that he just looked out for him, and he was his mother's Pastor, he felt obligated. He was already prepared for a comeback statement if the Pastor started asking him questions.

Curtis saw two empty seats in the corner and led the Pastor to them.

"What's up, Pastor, what's on your mind?" questioned Curtis.

"Truthfully, I just want to know how you are doing? You and the other young folks from the church like Devonte, Amani, Randy, Michelle, Farrah, Tasha, Evelyn, and the others who I remember when they were babies, are now grown adults. I consider you guys like my own kids. If anyone, including yourself needs help, please come talk to me."

Curtis sat back in his seat. "Wow, I never thought about it like that. You were there when the majority of us were just in elementary school."

"Yeah! Heck, Amani is getting married next year, and Farrah will be having her third child in a couple of weeks."

"Third child? Wow! I used to have a crush on her," responded Curtis while putting the first bag of chips on the seat next to him.

"Yeah, I just wish her, and this man would finally see fit to get married and stop living like they are married."

"Thanks, Pastor, but I'm okay, no need to worry about me."

Pastor Houston grinned, patted Curtis' knee, then stood up.

"Ok, well, I'm glad you are good. I wanted to hear it from you myself."

Curtis turned his lips sideways; eyebrows arched. "That's it, no discussion of the church, God, or you reciting Bible verses?"

"Are you going through something?"

"Um no, but...."

Pastor Houston shook his head, referencing no.

"Naw, see I learned a long time ago as a Pastor, that if someone wants to open up, they will. If they need to find me, they will. Like the old saying goes, pressure bursts pipes. So if someone needs help, you better say something."

Curtis nodded his head in agreement.

"There are a few reasons that people will open up to me. Either they feel guilty, there's evidence against them, or God will force you in a corner that you have to give it up. Curtis, all my children are grown. The young folks that I just mentioned to you a few minutes ago are grown now. The decisions they make, that's on them. I stop worrying about people who don't worry about themselves. All I can do is pray for them and ask God to allow one of his Angels to watch over them, and even with that, there's a time limit. You feel me?"

Pastor Houston went into his pocket, pulled out a business card and gave it to Curtis.

"I'm not hard to reach Curtis if you ever want to talk. But don't make it too late for the people who love you, to help you out," responded Pastor Houston.

Curtis just sat there. He wasn't expecting that response. He had his mind already pre-planned to combat all of Pastor Houston's holier than thou statements. But this time, he sat there for the first time in his life, feeling lonely, and didn't know what to do in his life. Everyone who could have been potential supporters, he damaged their relationship.

Pastor Houston headed out of the waiting area, and then made a drastic stop. He glanced over his shoulders.

"Hey Curtis, next time, stick and move my brother. And if that don't work, Run!"

Curtis gave him the thumbs up sign, and Pastor Houston left the waiting area headed toward Tasha's room.

Curtis sat, trying to finish off the last bags of chips. He licked the crumbs from each of his fingers, and then rubbed his fingers on the knee cap of his jeans to dry them off. When he looked up, he saw a man sitting next to a woman with his arms around her shoulder. The guilt of hurting Kyla sizzled within him. He finished his bag and laid it on the seat next to him. He pondered what would be his next move.

"I wish mama was here, she would know the right words to say," he whispered to himself.

He saw some newspapers on the table and grabbed one hoping to find the want ads to see if there were any new job openings. As usual, the same jobs listed. Either they don't pay enough, not qualified, too far away, or he didn't have any idea what to do at the job.

Once he couldn't find any newly available jobs, he laid the newspaper back on the table. Curtis closed his eyes, and tried his best to meditate, but the harder he tried, the chaos of today kept playing over and over in his mind -- images of Tasha lying in bed, the deep redness of Kyla's eyes when she confronted him about the woman's picture, Evelyn's constant questioning like he was in court, and then...

Curtis popped up, straight from his seat, opened his eyes, "DANG, I screwed up," Curtis emotionally and accidentally said out loud.

He looked around, and others in the waiting room were staring at him.

"I'm sorry, my bad guys... I just had a dream that the Boogeyman was after me," responded Curtis to the audience in the waiting room.

Some people in the waiting room giggled while others looked at him with disgust.

With all that happened to him today, Curtis realized that he was technically homeless. He got up and walked back to Tasha's room while trying to think of how he could fix the pieces to this crooked puzzle of his life.

Chapter Twelve

Dean, Rufus, Victor, and Ellis sat silently in the second pew in the hospital chapel on the bottom floor. Ellis was in the first pew, shaking his head, while the other men sat behind him. Looking at the statue of Jesus Christ on the cross hanging above them, Ellis mumbled, "Why, why is everything to me?" With a spirit torn out of his soul, and confidence drained, Ellis's eyes flushed, thinking of his family. "God, please help me!"

"Hey, we're here for you, you don't have to go through this alone," responded Rufus.

"Exactly," stated Victor, who was happy to know his friend was doing a little better.

"I know, I know, but thank you for being here," asserted Ellis.

Dean patted him on the shoulders. "It will be okay, man, and we'll get you through it."

"I hope so. I mean, I just don't know," Ellis responded.

"Stop being so hard on yourself; you did good! Many folks with college degrees wish they were on your level," commented Dean.

"But why do I feel like a failure? Huh, why do I feel like a failure?" Ellis asked while turning around to face Dean.

"My first child still hates me because when she was a teenager, with no job, no high school diploma, she ended up sneaking around and got pregnant. I told her she had to get rid of it. Despite my wife trying to tell me to let her keep it, that child wasn't in a position to raise a child."

Ellis turned his head toward Victor. "I can't be in a room with my one and only son without him hating me. For years we never were able to communicate without an argument. I always wondered why. Lately, I'm wondering was I that bad of a father. And out of all the people on the planet, he witnessed the worst thing that I've ever done. I still cannot believe that I put my hands on my wife! Yes, I hit her, and I can't say that it was an accident. It only happened one time, but I live with that memory every second I breathe. She cheated on me with someone. I wish I only knew why she did it. But after I struck her, I apologized to Gladys, and I swore that I would never bring it up."

Victor turned his head toward the other men, shocked about what Ellis confessed.

"I miss my wife; Lord knows I do! With all that I'm dealing with, Curtis hatred toward me, Tasha's attempted suicide, and Evelyn's attitude, I'd rather be dead. How bad I want my wife; it still scars me to know she cheated on me! And yeah, maybe I lead her into cheating. Maybe I wasn't there enough when she needed me. And I was just focused on the business and making money. Yeah, I can blame myself. But she didn't have to hurt me."

Ellis turned around and stared at the statue of Jesus Christ on the cross and then tilted his head down and stared at the wood, brown floors. "The funny thing, Tasha, is the only one of my children who really wants my time and really wants to talk to me. Yeah, she was acting funny lately. But growing up, she wanted to be around daddy. Yeah, I swore that I would never mention it to Gladys. But when I see Tasha, I always wonder if she is my child. I wonder a lot. Though I love her, it's just that thought that lingers with me."

Rufus got up and sat beside Ellis and held him in his arm. "Ellis, stop being so hard on yourself. You made decisions that you believed right. We all had to make tough decisions. Like Dean said, you're being too hard on yourself, and yes that is your child. You need to learn to let go and move forward in life, Ellis," Rufus explained.

Ellis shook his head. "I wish it was that easy; I wish I could believe you. My youngest child tried to commit suicide. Heck, I could have said something that may have prevented this. But I didn't. For years, my wife had some questions about her. But I just didn't focus on it. Yeah, I disregarded it! Not just because, but I ignored it because I have always thought that Tasha wasn't my child! When I see her, I think of my wife's infidelity! And that still scars me."

"What?" responded Victor.

The men looked at each other in confusion. Ellis felt the warm heat from their breaths of disbelief.

A small tapping sound drifted from the back. Dean turned and saw a young man trying to keep quiet while trying to get seated. Dean nodded his head toward the young man while the young man waved at him.

Victor turned around and then whispered into Ellis' ear, "I see you have a visitor."

"Hey fellas, let's get out and get some fresh air," Victor suggested.

Victor stood up and headed for exit, and the rest of the men strolled out of the chapel.

Ellis lifted his head. "If you want an apology or argument, then you might as well sit back there in silence or just leave me alone!"

Hearing his father, Curtis sat there in silence. He stared up at the statue and then closed his eyes. Dreams of his younger days surfaced, and the time he couldn't wait to see his father suffer in pain -- pain that only God could have helped him that he deserved for the way he treated his wife, family, and how he was a dictator.

Only if Dad knew, I was the one who wanted to make him suffer. Dad, you didn't know that a month after him attacking mama, I took all of my savings and bought a gun from the streets. And practiced how I would shoot you and when.

When Curtis had the opportunity, his Dad was asleep on the couch. His gun was loaded, and he wrote his name on the bullet. The gun was in his hand; the adrenaline of the steel rushed throughout his body. He felt no compassion, no love, or sympathy -- only revenge. He walked up to him, with the gun in his hand, making the mistake by turning around. When he turned, he saw those pretty brown eyes like his mama's, as Tasha stared at him.

Without saying a word, her glare said it all.

Curtis' arms shook and his anger turned to thought, which led to reasoning. *I can't kill my father.*

Later, Curtis threw the gun in the river, hoping it would sink so far in the water that no one would find it! Most importantly, hoping he didn't regret not pulling it.

Curtis opened his eyes, which were red as an apple. He stared at the statue of Jesus Christ on the cross and laughed. He got up and walked to his father and sat next to him.

Ellis' head adjusted left as his eyes tilted to the side. He looked over and saw his son cheesing like he was about to take a picture. "What got you smiling like you're drunk?" asked Ellis.

"I was just thinking about mama," responded Curtis.

"Oh," replied Ellis.

"Looking at this statue, I can hear mama saying to 'Keep God first, let's pray about it, Jesus this, Jesus that, in these types of situations.' She's right, you know?" stated Curtis.

Ellis struggled while trying to attempt a smile. "Oh yeah, she was a holy woman. She had a million statements and philosophies. I didn't know if she made it up or took it from somebody."

"Maybe a little bit of both," responded Curtis.

Ellis shook his head in agreement. He looked over at his son and was shocked that they were in the same room for more than three minutes, and a grenade hadn't gone off.

"Yeah, we often didn't listen to her until something bad happens. Like, when we were coming up, Evelyn was driving like she was on the Autobahn, but she forgot to put gas in her car. And like mama always say, 'Never drive your car on empty, because you never know when it's an emergency, and you shouldn't be wasting time at the gas station.' Mama always had a way of being right," Curtis stated.

"I violate that all the time," Ellis confessed.

Curtis grinned and nodded his head in agreement. "If I had a car, I would probably do the same," admitted Curtis.

Trying to show his father that he is holding up, but deep inside, his heart felt like it took a third-degree burn. Unaware that he heard most of his father's comments, Curtis wanted to scream, wanted to yell at him, and wanted to get some other stuff off his chest, but that moment he realized how much he was like his father -- both with no patience, both like to have control, and both were suffering from missing a special person.

With the issue facing his sister, Curtis wondered did he love Kyla because the thought of her has been surfacing in his mind. Curtis laid back on the pew and started daydreaming.

Ellis looked over to his son and wondered, *What the hell has Curtis gotten himself into with that bruised up face.*

"So, what's on your mind? You got quiet all of a sudden," asked Ellis.

Curtis popped out of his daydream, wishing he could go back. There, his thought of getting Kyla back was hopeful.

Ellis looked toward his son; even if he didn't have the scars, it was quite evident through his eyes and bumpy skin that he was suffering.

"Well, I just have a lot on my mind." Curtis nodded his head and turned his body back forward.

"Hey, let's go back upstairs. I was going to mention it until I saw your senior friends, that Tasha was just waking up, and Pastor was leading a prayer," said Curtis.

Ellis turned his head up in the air, "Thank you, Jesus, Thank you." Ellis turned toward Curtis and slapped him on his leg.

"Yeah, before Pastor started his one-room revival, I

dipped out to look for you. I thought his Deacon might want to join in on the program," said Curtis.

Ellis got up, stretching his arms.

"Okay, let's go up and check on your sister," responded Ellis.

Curtis stood beside his father. "Yes sir, let's see about your daughter."

Ellis grinned. "Okay, but by the way, since we have to pass the cafeteria, maybe you could ask one of the ladies who work there to stick your head in the ice machine. I mean we got to make sure that pretty face is together."

"You got jokes now?" responded Curtis.

Chapter Thirteen

Ellis closed his eyes and said a silent prayer of forgiveness of his behavior hoping that his baby girl would get back well and then wiped his hands to wipe the tears that ran down his face.

"Are you alright, Daddy?" Evelyn asked while she sat back in the chair; head tilted to the right while Curtis massaged her left shoulder with his right hand.

Ellis slowly turned his neck toward his two oldest children.

"You know what? You guys should go home and rest and come back in the morning," suggested Ellis, not knowing the war that his son had endured earlier that day.

Evelyn smiled and nodded her head while reaching for her purse.

Curtis stood with a frown on his face and eyes wide open. "Naw, I'm good," responded Curtis. "I should be here, be here for Tasha!"

With his hand diving in his pocket, Ellis walked up to Curtis, pulled out his keys, then proceeded to take off his house key so he could give it to him. "Here you go, son," responded Ellis while handing his son his house key.

Curtis shook his head and then waved his hand toward his father. "I'm good! You can go!"

"You need to get some rest unless your lady friend is

coming to pick you up from the hospital," said Ellis.

Curtis stopped waving. Ellis extended his arm, with his hand holding the key to give it to Curtis.

"I understand about needing some rest. But I'm good! For real! I need to be here for Tasha," replied Curtis.

Ellis stood motionless, arm slowly lowered. Evelyn walked up and grabbed the house key out of her fathers' hand and then stood beside her brother. Curtis looked down as Evelyn rubbed his arms, then her gripping, brown, eyes caught him. Beads of sweat formed on his brow and his heart beat faster. Evelyn presented a look that his mother used to give him when he knew he was in trouble, and he better straighten up.

"He's good, Daddy! We'll see you in the morning," Evelyn quickly stated while pulling her brother alongside her out of the room.

***

On the ride to his fathers' house, Curtis glared at the open scenery on the highway. While at the red light, Curtis snapped out of his trance, reminded that he was homeless while watching in pure sadness a woman rummaging through the trashcan and nibbling off what she pulled out. "I got to get my life in order," Curtis mumbled.

***

It just turned 1:00 a.m.

Ellis stood at the window, right arm leaning on the wall, while he examined the pitch-black sky and the glowing moon that reminded him of a new, shiny penny.

Ellis shook his head, trying to avoid the negative thoughts slowly creeping into the inside. *Oh, Lord! I wish Gladys were here. I wish she were here to deal with this instead of me.*

While the blinds were open, and the moonlight lit the room, Ellis grabbed the chair that Evelyn moved next to Tasha's bed. He sat, removed his shoes, slid them under the chair, and attempted to get comfortable in the seat. Ellis pulled out his cell phone from his pocket and wanted to read up on the national news on-line, but his phone was dead, and he forgot that he left his charger at the house. With his mind wandering and nerves in a panic mode, he went back to staring out the window until his eyes gradually closed, and the only thing he looked at was the dark caves of the back of his eyelids. Ellis slowly opened his eyes to a familiar scene in which he was the star.

***

In his office at the funeral home, Ellis talked on the phone, leaning back in his leather, black chair, legs crossed, while listening to one of his financial advisors. Ecstatic on what his financial advisor was telling him, plus the many bodies the funeral home was burying this weekend, Ellis was excited about his future fortune.

Bang, Bang, struck his office door interrupting his celebration. Gladys burst in and slammed the door behind her as she stomped toward her husband.

Startled, Ellis popped his head up, while still balancing the phone on the side of his face.

Ellis grabbed his phone and pressed it on his chess. "Do

you know that this is a place of business?"

"And… We need to talk!" With her hands on her hips, an attitude on her shoulders, and a tongue that was ready to strike, Gladys stood right in front of Ellis' desk.

Ellis turned his head away and put the phone back at his ear. "My bad… where were we again?"

Ellis looked down at his wall and glanced over and noticed Gladys was still in the same posture and assuming she is not leaving any time soon. He turned his head toward her, with his index finger in the air, he silently spoke, "Three minutes."

With a mean frown on her face, "No! We need to talk now Ellis! Get off the phone, Now!" Gladys sprinted toward the phone outlet, grabbed the cord, and yanked it out of the socket.

"I was having a good day until this!" *What the heck does she want?*

"Hello… Hel…" Ellis looked up, dropped the phone on the floor, and sat up in his chair. "So, what's the emergency, Gladys? Huh? That was an important call!"

"You know what the problem is!"

"If I knew the freaking problem, I wouldn't be asking! Once again, Gladys, what's the emergency?"

"Your daughter is the emergency! Your daughter has been asking for you! You're supposed to take her to a play today at her school? And don't give me that oh I forgot crap, Ellis! Cause we both know if something is important to you. You will make time for it!"

"So, you got me off the phone for that! A school play? I

thought it was a real emergency!"

"That is your child who wants to spend some time with you! Father-daughter time Ellis! You know, the thing that I've been trying to tell you to do with your other kids! But for some reason, this child would rather spend time with you than to play with her friends!

Ellis reviewed several documents in a folder on his desk. "I never said I was going to take her. You may have suggested to her that I would, but I never co-sign to do that!"

"You got the audacity to sit your ass in that seat and act like this is no big deal. I… I just don't understand you!"

"Hell… I can say the same thing about you, Gladys! You're yelling and being ignorant in my place of business! You're trying to make me feel guilty of something that I didn't or don't want to do. Hell, I do not want to go to some school play. If it was that important, you should take her. I don't know why you try to force me to go to things that I don't care for nor have the time to waste. I got better things to do with my time!"

"That's your child! Can you for once give her some love and attention? That's all I'm saying, Ellis! Stop thinking about our issues and focus on her!"

Ellis looked up toward Gladys. "You sure?"

Gladys hardened her stance, slowly shaking her head, and her lips poked out! "Is that it?" Gladys trembled, wiping her eyes. "One day Ellis, I pray that God will hit you on the head, so you can just wake up and see how much of an butthole you are! And it could hit you here… in your business. I guess what I do ain't nothing! Consoling those who lost someone is not helpful."

"Wait, Gladys! I didn't mean it like that…"

"...You used to have a loving heart, but I guess money, and a big title like Chairman of the Deacon Board changed you."

Ellis stood behind his desk, glancing over at their wedding picture on the corner of his desk. "Are you done? I was having a good day until this crap! Speaking of praying, pray not to be promiscuous again. How about that?"

Gladys turned around and hurried out. She grabbed the doorknob and without mercy, slammed the door leaving a stiff breeze that sent the documents flying and picture frames shaking.

Ellis dropped down onto his seat, watching all of his paperwork fly throughout the office. "Oh, well!"

Ellis got up and retrieved his paperwork off the floor.

"How the hell is she's going to get mad at me for not wanting to be around her. She was the one fooling around," Ellis said to himself out loud. "I don't believe Tasha's my child! She can't be!"

Ellis kneeled, and his grumbling got louder and louder while picking up the scattered documents on the floor.

Hearing a slight movement, "What is it now?" he said, thinking it's Gladys for round two. He looked up and saw Tasha, in her yellow and blue dress, with tears dropping like hourglass sand wishing her daddy would be her date.

"Oh, God! Don't tell me." With his mouth open, Ellis slowly inhaled while feeling his heart tumbling from his chess. *"Don't tell me that she heard me all this time."*

Tasha's eyes filled with tears, she frowned as she stared at the floor as if watching her shattered heart fall on the ground!

"No! No! No!" yelled Ellis. "Tasha, please don't cry."

Tasha glared toward her father and then bolted.

"No, no, no, no, no! I'm sorry... I'm sorry!"

"Daddy, Daddy! Just die!"

"UGH!!!" screamed Ellis, who popped up his seat with sweat running down his face like rain.

***

"Dad, are you alright? Should I call the nurse," Tasha calmly asked.

Ellis fought to catch his breath. "Wow, that was a dream!"

Tasha turned her hospital bed light on.

"Seems more like you had a nightmare. Do you need me to call the nurse for you?"

Ellis stood up. "I'm good. Give me one minute to get myself together, Tasha," he said while walking toward the bathroom.

He turned on the bathroom light, looked toward the mirror ashamed of himself. Shaking his head, he took several paper towels and wiped his face. He sat on the side of the tub.

The bathroom lights clicked off, and Ellis walked out.

Tasha wiped her eyes. She left the bedrail lights on, so her father wouldn't have to use the light of the moon to maneuver in the room.

Tasha raised the head of the bed. Surprised to see her father in the room, she watched him pace toward his seat. Ellis fell back into the chair, rubbed the armrest, and began smiling at Tasha.

Both of their eyes met, but Tasha quickly pulled away.

"So, where's Curtis?" Tasha asked.

"I told him that he could stay at my house to rest." Ellis stood up and walked to the foot of the bed. "By the way, his face was looking... it looked like he needed it. Looks like he took a pretty good beating."

"What? Um, is Evelyn here, or is she in the lobby?

"I told her to get some rest too. Both should be here in the morning. I would call, but my phone is dead, and I left the charger at the house."

"So, you're saying that it's just you and me here?" Tasha asked while frowning.

Ellis walked toward Tasha and stood over her. "Yes, I wanted to make sure you are good." Ellis put his hand on top of Tasha's hand; she quickly jerked her hand back.

Stunned, Ellis stepped back from the bed, having his left heel to hit the chair leg. He turned around and sat down in the chair. He looked up, and Tasha had laid her head on the pillow on the opposite side while lying back in the bed.

Ellis tilted his head and closed his eyes. *I wish Gladys were here. She would have known what to do.*

"Tasha, so how are you feeling? Is there anything I can do to help?"

Tasha lay there quietly like she didn't hear the words from her father.

"So, Tasha, how are you feeling?" Ellis asked again.

"Why do you ask? You never cared about me?"

Ellis sat like a lost child in a store. Struggling to figure out what he should say to start a meaningful dialogue, he closed his eyes once again and leaned back on the chair.

"I'm sorry! Tasha, I'm sorry!"

Tasha opened her eyes and turned her head toward him staring at him. With her glossy eyes and her emotions spinning, Tasha trembled in shock because she had never in her life heard her father use any apologetic words toward her.

"All my life, I always wanted you to be there for me. But all I had was a dream. It was just a stupid dream of my father wanting to be there for his baby girl. Mom always made excuses for you on why you couldn't do this or how you acted. Eventually, it got to the point I felt like it was the same blah, blah, blah, crap!"

Ellis opened his eyes to listen to his daughter.

"I know I'm not special. I miss Mom because she made me feel important. I could tell her anything, and she would be there for me. I didn't really have any true friends growing up. The only person besides Mom that had my back was Curtis. He was the reason why I live, until he disappeared. He was my shepherd. He was my inspiration. Without him, I probably would have already tried to kill myself!"

Ellis lifted his head and turned toward Tasha.

"I knew you didn't love me. I always told myself that you did. But I was tired of lying to myself." Tasha studied her arms to examine her past wounds.

Ellis walked toward the window to glance out. He wiped his eyes and shook his head. "Tasha... Um, see, your Mother and I had issues. And..."

"...I know, Dad! Mother had a temporary fling. She told me. Eventually, we had that talk. As she said, she wanted to get things off her chest, in case she lost her battle to cancer."

Ellis sat back and remained quiet. For the first time in a long time, his ears remained opened for whatever would come from Tasha.

"She told me that she regretted it and... you made sure that she didn't forget!

Listening to Tasha's pain jerked his hurt. His selfish ways blinded him to the fact that she loved and adored him. Ellis knew there were no words that could help ease the drama from the past. All he has now was this moment and the future.

"I'm sorry, so sorry, Gladys," Ellis mumbled between short breaths.

Ellis turned around and went toward Tasha with his head and heart hanging down. "I'm sorry. I shouldn't have hurt you! I was hurt and torn by your mother's action. And that had nothing to do with you."

Tasha reached over to pull out a few pieces of Kleenex from the dresser. "So, what's next? Do you want to find out if I am your child?"

"There's no need. You're my child!"

Ellis embraced Tasha. "Whatever I can do to help you, we'll get through it."

Chapter Fourteen

"These dag-on traffic got me late," Ellis said to himself while pulling up to Mom and Pop Bar-B-Que restaurant. He looked at the restaurant and didn't know if it was a porta potty or storage house.

Ellis got out the car, and the aroma of barbecue chicken pinched his nose. He strolled toward the restaurant; as his head moved side to side like windshield wipers. The slightest little noise made him overly cautious. *I hope I don't get robbed up here.*

Pushing his key lock twice, Ellis walked in and saw Rufus already had them a table in the corner.

"Hey," Rufus announced while embracing Ellis with a handshake and hug. Rufus wore his black suit, white shirt, and red tie, which was apparent that he attended a funeral earlier in the day.

"Sorry I'm late, this traffic is crazy. It seems like everywhere I turned, construction was going on," stated Ellis.

"You good." I was still trying to decide what I would like to eat," responded Rufus, who reviewed the index-card-sized menu.

From the first scent, Ellis knew that he wanted to try some of that barbecue chicken. Though this restaurant wasn't a big place, the best types of foods come from a hole in a wall. Both men waited patiently for the waitress to take their drink orders.

"How's the family?" asked Rufus, who was looking like a movie star with dark shades on.

"We are making it. That's all I can say. Tasha is good; she's getting the help that she needs. Evelyn is looking to go on a cruise next week, so I may go in to help run the business, and I invited Curtis to stay with me until he gets his priorities in order."

"Dang!"

"Yeah, I'm learning to keep my mouth closed and to choose my battles wisely," mentioned Ellis, who was waiting on the waitress to bring him a cup of water.

"Good! Good to hear." Rufus dug into his jacket pocket and pulled out an obituary and laid it in the middle of the table.

Ellis picked it up and read the program, wondering which funeral home serviced them. Emma Ivey was her name, and she passed away two weeks ago. "I wonder if she had insurance and was that the reason for the late burial."

"Before you start going all Columbo over there, Emma's husband is named Jesse Ivey, and she died of lung cancer," Rufus reported.

Ellis shook his head. "I don't know if it will ever happen in my lifetime, but I wish there could be a cure for this disease."

Rufus nodded his head in agreement. Within minutes, the waitress brought both men cups of water, and took their orders.

Ellis grabbed his cup and gulped down the cup of water as if in a drinking competition.

Rufus looked at him and then decided to push his water over to his side of the table.

"Whoa, that was good, cold, and refreshing," Ellis testified.

"Yeah, I can tell that you were might thirsty," acknowledged Rufus.

Ellis signaled the waitress to come over while pointing at his cup. "So, I see that you are recruiting a new man for the team, but how's the rest of the crew?"

"Everyone is doing well. Victor got to have hip surgery in two days," added Rufus.

"Oh, yeah, I forgot about that; he will surely be in my prayers," stated Ellis, who rubbed his belly.

Rufus stood up, took off his jacket, and hung it up on his chair. Ellis looked over the obituary program and slid it back to Rufus.

Rufus sat back down scooting his chair next to Ellis. "I admire you, Ellis!" Rufus put his arm over Ellis' shoulder.

Before Rufus could say any more... "Move back, now!" demanded Ellis. "Hey, hey, we are cool, but not that cool," Ellis responded while pushing his arm off of his shoulder.

"Wait! That's not what I meant," Rufus tried to explain.

"You better clarify," stated Ellis, who didn't care about the many eyes, staring at his direction.

Rufus moved his chair back over and grabbed his cup of water and took two big gulps.

Ellis put both of his elbows on the table, his right hand clenched a fist, while the left hand palmed his right hand.

"For all that you been through lately, from your wife and your kids, not too many people could handle it as well as you did. And it took courage to admit your wrongs. That's what I meant," responded Rufus.

"You sure?" asked Ellis.

"Yes, come on now, Ellis," stated Rufus.

"Um, thank you. I don't know what to say. I just had to deal with the hand I was given. I'm sorry for pushing you. I didn't know what to expect," replied Ellis.

Rufus nodded his head.

The waitress brought two more cups of water and announced that the food should be coming real soon.

"My mistake for getting in your space; however, I did want to inform you."

"You're good!"

Rufus smiled and then looked up. He put his head back down, opened his mouth, but words failed to come out. It was like he tried to put a sentence together, but it kept coming out as a fragment.

Ellis kept calm but steadily looked at his friend. Rufus then took off his shades, and there were enough bags around his eyes for a month's trip to Africa. Rufus grabbed his cup and gulped the remaining water. Seconds later, he grabbed the cup again and shoved the ice cubes into his mouth.

"You said something at the hospital, that I can truly feel. As a matter of fact, I can understand. We both have experienced pain that we often blame on ourselves," mentioned Rufus.

"Okay," Ellis stated while leaning back in his chair.

Rufus leaned forward on the table. "Today would've been my dear Anita's birthday if she was living. So, I woke up with her on my mind. Hopefully, I'm not acting too emotional."

"Well, I understand, Gladys' birthday is in three weeks."

Rufus sat back, looking around the restaurant. "In my younger days, I was what people now would call a player. But truly, I was a whore. I couldn't stay faithful if you paid me. Even in my marriage, I dipped in and out of my relationship. I tried to be fully faithful, but it was like an addiction. Trust me, my wife Anita satisfied me, and I loved her more than I can say, but just that taste of another woman excited me."

Ellis looked up and saw the waitress coming and stopped Rufus before he said another word.

"I see them plating your food, and it should be back in a minute," the waitress mentioned.

Both men shook their heads and smiled until the waitress walked right past them to another table. Both men's stomachs growled.

"Get back to the story, at least it can distract me from my hungry belly," demanded Ellis.

"Well, a few years back, someone I used to mess with named Gwen, well, I guess you can say she used to be my side girl for a while; I received a call that she was rushed to the hospital. Hell, I didn't even know that she was sick. I'm not a hospital type of person. I was hoping to see her when she got out, but I was told that I needed to be there and be there as soon as possible. So, I went, not knowing what was going on. I went into the room, I saw her sister and niece in the room sitting down, and my heart slipped out of my body. She was there with needles sticking everywhere and a mask to help her to breathe. For a moment, I stood there like a mannequin. Gwen saw me, and we usually greeted each other by pointing our middle finger in the air. But that's another story of itself."

The waitress brought out the food, and both men prayed over it. Ellis requested two cups of water and hot sauce.

"Her sister and niece walked out of the room, and I grabbed one of the chairs and placed it right next to the bed. In my mind, I'm still trying to put things together. I was assuming it was her sickle cell. Before I said anything, she came out and told me that she had something called AIDS."

Ellis stopped chewing, quickly swallowed the pieces of chicken in his mouth and was about to ask the question before Rufus insisted on letting him finish the story.

"She told me that I wasn't the only guy she danced with. The only major difference is that the other guy gave me a gift that I can never exchange," reminisced Rufus.

"Woo!" responded Ellis while wiping his mouth from the rich sauce sticking to his face.

Nodding his head while looking over his food, and just before he took his first bite, "Yeah, that's how I felt. The next morning she died around seven. I loved that woman. Besides losing my mother and brother from the war, this was the first time in a long time that I got slapped so hard; it left an imprint like a fossil. I swear, I think about her at least two to three times a week."

Ellis stopped eating and said nothing. It was like he was cotton-mouthed, but he just flooded his mouth with barbecue sauce, hot sauce, and his fifth cup of ice-cold water. While coming up in the mortuary business, he was targeted by many women but didn't want to be branded as a sapsucker.

"Later on that morning, I saw my wife walking downstairs, and she started coughing, which was odd to me because she rarely gets sick. I mean, I can probably count on my fingers the times she was sick. She goes to the gym, eats healthy, and she doesn't smoke. Ellis, someone always says that karma will pay you back if you do someone wrong, but I never let those talks worry me! But that moment, if my wife caught something or something happen to her because of my actions, hell, I would probably jump off a bridge without hesitation. So that morning, I called the doctor, and just my luck someone had just canceled their appointment that day, so I took it."

Rufus looked over at Ellis and noticed that there were only three bites of his chicken, a full load of fries still on his plate, and coleslaw hadn't been touched.

"I hope I'm not making you uncomfortable," Rufus said.

Ellis sat with his arms crossed, mouth tucked in, trying to put his thoughts together not to portray the angry man who was cheated on.

"I appreciate you for sharing, but it bothers me that you cheated on your wife. If you wanted to mess around, why not just be single?"

"I thought I was untouchable. Bullets could be busting at me but would intentionally bypass me and hit someone else. Call it a curse, but I always had that power," Rufus confessed.

Ellis grabbed a fork full of coleslaw and placed it in his mouth. Rufus wasn't the first person that he knew with the gift of P.O.P, but better known as the Power of Persuasion. People like Rufus used his looks and personality to get what they wanted and what others desired.

"So, I went to the doctor, I got checked up, and the doctor gave me the best news that I have heard in a long time. I was in good condition! No disease, no issue!" Rufus looked up in the air and pointed at the sky. "Thank you, God! All he suggested for me was to exercise more and drink more water."

"That was a blessing," Ellis acknowledged.

Rufus smiled and gave Ellis a fist pump. "Yes, it was! And that day, I promised myself that I would never do anything to put myself, my wife, or anyone that I'm close to in harm's way. As I said, I don't know if I could have lived with myself."

"That's good!" Ellis felt his phone vibrating, and it was his wife's cousin Jerry. "Dang, either he calls me when it's not the right time, or I totally forget to call him back."

Rufus smiled, and then slowly, his smile deceased. He picked up a french fry, took a bite, and placed it back on his plate.

Ellis glanced at his friend, assuming that this was about to be the toughest part he would have to discuss.

"I got off work early and went to my brother's house to help him fix his toilet. Once we were done, I wanted to hurry up home because Anita told me that morning that she was cooking my favorite dinner of fried chicken, collard greens, and cornbread. While fixing that toilet, the thought of her well-seasoned fried chicken had me needing a sponge to soak up the drool."

Ellis sniggled while attempting to take a bite of his barbecue chicken.

"Soon as we were done, I quickly headed to my car to leave. Soon as I stepped into my car, it started sprinkling. When I drove about a mile down the street, it started pouring down with mean aggression. Normally I would have gone fifty, but the showers were blurring my view. I had to go twenty-five, blinkers on, and I had to rely on the yellow lines to guide me home. Finally, I got home, and I rushed out of my car like I was a running back, with an open hole, and seeing the goal line for the touchdown. Before I could even touch the doorknob, it popped open without any hesitation. I stepped inside, believing that I was at home, but seconds later, I found myself inside of a military trench about to go to war. No smell of friend chicken welcomed me home, and before I could say, Anita, she slapped my chest with a letter."

"Sounds intense."

"Oh, it was! She screamed, 'You cheater, how could you?' I didn't know what to say. I snatched the letter from her. Anita and I had our disagreements before, but the only time we ever yelled at each other was when she snuck five hundred out of my account to help her drug addict sister. She just stood there, without any emotions. Those brown, loving eyes of hers were switched to hurt and pain. I started reading it, and I couldn't believe the lines, the words, the message, and whom it was coming from. That second, I felt like I was dreaming and was hoping someone would shake me to get me out of this nightmare. I tried to keep my composure, but Anita was breathing hot fire, and I didn't have an extinguisher. I might as well say that I'm guilty and deal with my punishment, but oftentimes pride can make a simple decision more difficult."

The waitress came by to check on the men. Rufus stopped telling the story, and Ellis informed the waitress that they were both doing well. The waitress smiled and walked away. Ellis sat back and was awaiting the remainder of Rufus' soap opera.

"As I mentioned, this was a nightmare. I just stood reading it line by line over and over again. I still couldn't believe what I was reading. Anita was still in my face; then, out of nowhere, she put her finger about an inch from my face. I looked down at her; she started backing up. Anita wasn't crazy, she knew that was one of my pet peeves, and if you crossed that line, then you force me to battle. Anita started screaming and crying. Her five-foot frame started shaking, so she stormed into the living room and sat. I stood there without a word to say. I was so zoned out that I didn't see the lightning making music in the sky, the rain overflowing outside, and most importantly, I didn't see the door wide open until Anita snatched her purse from the floor and stood by the door. 'I... I... I... got to, got to go,' Anita stuttered. Just coming from outside, and as a seasoned driver, it was difficult for me to come home. I knew she shouldn't be out there. She should be here with me. I should be apologizing. I should be confessing and asking God for forgiveness, but I didn't say a word. Anita walked out the door without looking back. I should have run after her, but all I did was just walk to the door, watch her jump in her car and go. Maybe she was going to her coworker's house down the street. She should be okay, I figured. After witnessing her drive off, I just walked in the living room with this letter in my hand, heart dragging on the floor, and mind on a temporary hiatus. I sat down and went over the letter again."

Rufus wiped his hands, then went into his pocket like he

was scavenger hunting, pulled out a letter, put it on the table, and pushed it forward.

Ellis grabbed a napkin and wiped his mouth and hands, and then he gently picked up the letter. Within seconds Ellis' head kept popping up and down from reading, with amazement and shock. Like a tire spinning, Ellis kept on reading. It was to the point that he could remember the lines like he was he about to rehearse for a movie. Ellis couldn't help but to think that in life, there are certain quotes that never get old, like those that are aimed to inspire a person.

When someone has a lot on their plate, someone may quote, "How do you eat an elephant? One bite at a time." When it comes to relationships, every man needs to know Hell hath no fury as a woman scorned.

"Dear Anita Dennis,

My name is Gwen Hampton. We have never formally met, but I've heard several stories about you from your husband, Rufus Dennis. Not only was I told that you were a beautiful person inside, but outside as well. I can honestly admit that I was jealous of you.

You are probably wondering why I am not speaking to you face-to-face or why I wrote a letter and had it mailed to you. Well, if you are reading this letter, I have taken my last breath on Earth and hoping that my soul has found an eternal resting place with the Lord. I've done a lot of things in my life. Some moments that I'm happy about, a few that were bad, and some that I regret and even when I write this, I'm steadily wiping the tears from my eyes.

I've made a few decisions in my life that I shouldn't

have. Knowing that the hourglass sand is slowly vanishing for me, I want to make some confessions, and hopefully, God will forgive me.

Before your marriage and often within, Rufus and I had an affair. He will have to explain why he wanted to see me, but for me, he was the ideal type of man for me. I guess he didn't see me more than a potential mate, but I accepted it. Since I couldn't have Rufus to myself, I played the field, and unknowingly dealt with someone that gave me a gift that would forever change my life. I was given AIDS. Before I passed away, I told Rufus. I can't imagine him telling you or how to tell you. So, I found out where he lived, and I wanted to personally tell you this.

-Gwen

Chapter Fifteen

Ellis gripped the letter staring at Rufus, who stopped eating and tapped his fork on the table; his lips poked out like a child after getting a whooping, and his eyes stared over Ellis' head.

"Wow," was the only thing Ellis stated while folding the letter and sliding it back toward his friend. He glanced at Rufus and shook his head before he finished scooping up the last bit of his coleslaw.

Rufus looked at Ellis while turning the folded letter in a circle with his index finger. "I sat back on my couch, holding this letter. I originally wanted to think of my next move, but the warm couch embraced me until it massaged me to sleep. I opened up my eyes and saw the moon waving at me. Feeling my stomach kicking my ribs, I got up and headed toward the kitchen to fix me a turkey sandwich, and looking toward the door, I didn't realize that I didn't shut it or even locked it. I opened the door, peaking outside while the cool breeze was kissing me all over my face -- no sign of Anita. Looking down at my watch, it was two something. My hunger quickly replaced by worry. Before I could have moved a step, the house phone rang. I ran to the phone and yanked it off the hook. Next thing I know, I was heading to Eagle Creek. When I arrived, I just sat there, thinking I was looking at a live TV show with no music on, but the sign of the engine running and my heart clapping like it's giving outstanding applause. One of the cops recognized me and approached my car. Gripping the stirring wheel, fumbling with the keys, I finally remembered how to turn the car off, but left my keys in the ignition. I slowly opened my car door and was quickly instructed to follow them. Legs shaking! I tried to keep up until I got my conclusion. A few of the local reporters just pulled up and started bursting out of their vans for the latest tragedy. Numbed. Muted. Grasping for air. The person who was laid on the gurney was my heart, my love, and my wife, my Anita."

"Wow!" Ellis wiped a tear from his eyes.

"I was told that Anita was driving about fifty-five miles an hour in that storm and when she was coming to a dead man's curve, she tried to hit the brakes but her car hydroplaned, and knowing Anita, she probably panicked which lead her to collide with a tree on the driver side, which was crushed and smashed like someone stepping on a can. They believe she died instantly on impact. My Anita…"

Rufus placed his hands over his eyes and tried to hold back his emotions.

The waitress walked up but stopped when Ellis put his index finger up. Ellis wanted to give Rufus sympathy, but his mind persuaded his heart not too. *He caused all this damage to himself.* The thought of Rufus helping him out, motivated Ellis to get up and rub Rufus' back.

Slowly breathing and wiping his face, Rufus gained his composure. He finally took the folded letter and put it in his shirt pocket. "Well, I brought Anita back here to be buried with her people. We both always said that if something ever happened to either of us, we wanted to be buried by our family. Since her passing, I was haunted by the fact that I should have made her stay home. I didn't say anything to her. I stood there like I was the victim! I cheated on her. Wow, I lied to God! I didn't follow my vows, and she ended up dying. Maybe that was my punishment. Felt like I was Job in the Bible. If you know what I mean."

Ellis nodded his head and gave a sly grin while leaning back in his seat. He didn't care to debate the two situations.

"Well, we actually used your business."

"Oh, okay!"

"My daughter Olivia and her husband organized the arrangement and funeral. Yeah, your daughter worked with us. She was so professional."

"Thank you. I taught her well." Ellis smiled while leaning back even further in his seat.

"The wake was at your funeral home. Looking at her in that silver casket, she looked just like she was sleeping. So gorgeous! So peaceful! I tried to be strong, but I couldn't. It felt like it was a rotation of friends and family members taking turns to take care of me. At the wake, I sat on the couch, which was located diagonally to her casket and just stared at her. There wasn't one word that someone said that could have extinguished my pain that evening until this mysterious woman pulled up a chair and sat next to me like she knew me."

"Yeah."

"Well, at first I didn't even realize someone was next to me. If you didn't know better, you would have thought I was dead. Motionless. Slow breathing. Cold body. Braindead. Hell, I could have fit well in one of your caskets."

"Trust me, I understand."

"My mind was in a black hole, and I wasn't keeping anything in. All that was on my mind was the guilt, the guilt I have to deal with for the rest of my life! You know, the guilt that's sticking to me like a fly in a spider web. I glanced over to her, and I could see her mouth moving, but to me, she was mute. I turned back around to look at my wife, but strangely for some reason, her words started tapping me on the head like a woodpecker to a tree. She, she was telling me that she knew that I loved her, and it was obvious that I have a pain that requires some internal healing. I turned to her, and I just started listening to her. Then I had to ask, could God truly forgive me with tears streaming down. She looked at me without any emotions. So I repeated myself, could God truly forgive me?"

Ellis felt his phone vibrating on his belt, so he pulled it out and glanced down. *Dang, Jerry was calling again.*

"Before she replied, she turned around and eyed the crowd, then slowly stood up, tapped me on the arm, and instructed me to follow her."

Ellis sat back up, moving forward placing his elbows on the table with his arms crossed curious to know where this conversation was leading too.

"At first, I didn't know what I should do. I've been sitting in that chair so long that my behind fell asleep. When I finally got up, I had to take some baby steps to try to get my rhythm. So, I followed her to the lobby. I tell you, Ellis, I never met this woman before in my life. I couldn't even tell you if she was part of your staff, family member, or someone off the street. So I met her in the lobby and went outside toward the parked limousines. She started pointing out to the sky, which was turning gray, and the stars were just emerging. She said, 'That regardless of what we have done, there's a man who sits high and looks low, who knows and understands our weakness.' She handed me this piece of paper to read, which I was paranoid to take. So reluctantly, I took it and read over it."

"What did it say?" asked Ellis.

"If we confess our sins, he is faithful and just to forgive us our sins and to cleanse us from all unrighteousness. It came from scripture in First John, Chapter 1, verse nine. She told me to read it every day, and don't be ashamed of my past because you would never know how it may help others. I looked at the woman, and she kept smiling like it was some type of happy occasion. I started rereading it, then began shaking my head and was about to begin walking back inside to the wake until I confessed to her what I had done. She stopped smiling, I figured, and I started walking back until she grabbed my arm. Before I could turn around, she confessed that she broke her vows and that her number one fan was crushed, and she truly didn't know if he honestly had forgiven her. I stood there for the moment, speechless. I was about to ask her something until I heard my daughter calling my name. 'Go on and see about your family,' she said."

Mouth wide open, Ellis sat up from his seat.

"Before I left, she wrote down her number and told me to give her a call tomorrow. I did, and every other day we spoke. She was kinda like my unofficial therapist. A few weeks later, she told me she was diagnosed with cancer, and she had surgery scheduled soon. She had a strange request. She claims it was the Holy Spirit talking to her. She asked me if I could look after her husband if she passed away. She wanted me to be his best friend. She knew that he didn't have a close relationship with his children, and he was stubborn as hell. I said yes, I mean, how could you say no to that request. Or, maybe I was caught up in the moment. Honestly, I didn't know or understand how I was going to do it. But life is funny, and things one at a time work itself out."

"Or times that we asked why things are the way they

are?" responded Ellis.

"So true!" Pointing at Ellis. "I don't have to tell you who was that angel."

Ellis just sat there, wanting to put a sentence together but not knowing how to start.

"In time, I lost contact with her. Which maybe it was for the best. Until I saw her picture in the obituary, I really wanted to let her know that the Bible verse helped me. I wanted to tell her thank you. Yeah, I'm not going to lie and say that I still don't blame myself. But it's easier to look at myself in the mirror. I truly feel that I have a purpose in my life, and I do feel that I lived up to my promise to her."

Ellis started smiling and nodding his head. "She was an amazing woman."

"So Ellis, when I told you at your wife's gravesite that I came to help you, and that I know you, I truly meant it. It wasn't by accident, my friend!"

Chapter Sixteen

BEEP! BEEP!

Ellis' head jerked while his eyes swayed side to side and his heart pumped like a balloon being pumped while the ice-cold nerves ran through him like a sprinter. He stomped on the accelerator like it was a roach, and then proceeded to go through the yellow light before it turned red. Looking through the rearview mirror, the man flipping the middle finger was understood. The words from Rufus stunned him like a wasp bite. He began to roll up his window and then turned on the AC. The cool air massaged his face while calming down the wet pores. The thoughts of the conversation were tiptoeing throughout his head and he nearly hit a pedestrian while crossing the street. Ellis pounded his brakes.

"IDIOT!" the pedestrian yelled while scurrying across the street while giving Ellis the middle finger!

Knowing he was wrong; Ellis took a loud sigh while trying to catch his breath. He looked at his rearview mirror and didn't see a car coming in his direction. Ellis drove a mile ahead, and instead of heading west toward his home, he went east to his future home.

Ellis pulled up to his destination. He turned off the engine, slowly opened the door, and walked the hill while staring out toward Gladys' grave. As soon as he approached the grave, he kissed the top of the tombstone, bent his knees, and then slowly sat on the grassy area next to the tombstone with his back facing the direction of his truck. Ellis stared at Gladys' name for the moment. Even though it had been months, the realization that she was gone still hurt him to the core.

"Baby, you make my heart smile," Ellis tearfully spoke.

He looked toward the sky, with both arms in the air with each of his index fingers pointing, "Thank you! God, you surely have an extraordinary angel in your midst."

He took three quick breaths. "I always loved you. Yes, we had our issues, but I miss you more than I can say. And you, just listening to Rufus, you still kept that scripture I gave you about forgiveness. Regardless of what you were dealing with, you tried to look out for me. I mean, for Godsakes, you were dealing with cancer!"

Ellis immediately closed his eyes, tilting his head down in a posture of prayer. From the eastern skies, a subtle breeze slowly rubbed through Ellis' hair, and a smile arose when he imagined him lying on Gladys' lap after a rough day, and her telling him that everything would be all right. Her smile, her majestic eyes, and the warmth of her love soothed and mended a broken spirit.

"I love you."

Ellis' eyes popped open like an ice-cold beer can when he heard a vehicle gently pulling in the parking lot. He looked over his shoulder and saw a familiar person stepping out of the car. He turned his neck back to Gladys' tombstone with his eyebrows arching up and started getting up, using the top of the tombstone as a prop to help him stand up straight. Kissing the top of the tombstone once again, Ellis dusted off his pants, and then pulled out his handkerchief and wiped his forehead.

"Hey there, I hope I wasn't disturbing you," asked Mrs.

Beverly, who carried carnations on her left arm and her purse on the right side.

"Oh, you are the one who has been placing those on the grave," Ellis stated while pointing toward the carnations.

Mrs. Beverly smiled while nodding her head. "Yes sir, I'm the culprit. I surely miss my friend and knew she loved these flowers."

"Yeah, she did love those flowers."

Mrs. Beverly approached the grave, put her purse on top of it, gave a one-arm hug to Ellis, and then laid the flowers in the middle of the grave. Ellis and Mrs. Beverly stood in silence, looking at the grave.

"You guys surely take care of your graveyard," Mrs. Beverly said looking around. "I went to visit my husband, and the gravesite was a mess. I could have cursed out those folks at the church.

"Oh yeah, we don't play that. For many of us, we got family, and close friends buried out here, so we…" Ellis paused while feeling the vibration of his cell phone. He pulled it off the clip and noticed it was his wife's cousin Jerry, which he had forgotten to return his call. He touched the green receiver button. "Hey Jerry, hold on one second for me, please." Ellis turned toward Mrs. Beverly. "Hey, I need to take this, you have a great day now."

"Okay," responded Mrs. Beverly.

Ellis hugged Mrs. Beverly and walked down the hill.

Mrs. Beverly watched Ellis walk until he got inside of his truck. She turned around and walked around Gladys' grave with a lukewarm expression. "I knew I didn't fully have his heart. I knew, I knew it was someone. But I didn't know it was you. I didn't know I played second fiddle to you. You had a dedicated husband, a family that loved you, but you had to have more. You smiled in my face, you pretended to be my friend, but on the side having an affair with my husband. I wondered why you told me that you love me and asked me to forgive you. If my husband weren't such a sloppy writer, I wouldn't have picked out his handwriting that I saw at your daughter's drawer. Hell, or should I say if he wasn't such a lazy writer, that same mess he wrote to you, he wrote the same thang to me! Line by line. Word for word. The same love letter. How could you?"

Mrs. Beverly's tears of hate ran down her face like melting lava. She pictured smashing Gladys' tombstone with a sledgehammer. She opened up her purse and pulled out a hammer, holding it tight like a bolt to a tire.

Ellis sat in his truck, with the key in the ignition, feeling guilty of not taking Jerry's calls, just sat there listening to Jerry talk about his new granddaughter Evonne Gladys Hampton.

"My grandbaby is so adorable. I gotta mail you guys some pictures."

"Sure, please do."

"Yeah, I'm going to miss my cousin. I requested my daughter to at least give my grandbaby the middle name of Gladys. Wait... while I'm thinking about it, what's so funny is the man you spoke about, the secret man you heard about, his wife was at the funeral."

"Huh, say that again."

"Yeah, Charlie Lee was his name. I remember when they

used to sneak out with each other. Her daddy didn't trust him, so he forbids her to see him. Of course, they still did until he had to leave out of town for the army. And you know her daddy didn't have her to leave. A couple of years ago, I came down home to visit, and I stopped by the funeral home. I spoke to Ala... something, but her last name, I believe, was Mrs. Beverly. Well, when I asked to see Gladys, I noticed the picture on her desk. He looked so familiar, but I didn't say anything to her. So when Gladys and I went to lunch, and I told her about the picture, at first, she didn't want to say anything, but then it hit me, it was that dude. I remember that birthmark on the top of his temple. So, she finally admitted to me that it was him. I didn't understand why she didn't say who he was when I first asked. It was like she was hiding something."

"What the Hell?" Ellis opened up his truck door, stepped out, and looked toward Mrs. Beverly, who held a hammer in her hand while pacing around Gladys' grave.

THE END.

About the Author
Trae D. Johnson

A Harlem, Georgia native, Trae D. Johnson is an author of fiction and nonfiction works and CEO of Campania Publishing, LLC. He enjoys writing books that can educate students, parents, and high school counselors as well as creating imaginary works of art that draw you into the characters and the story. He and his wife, LaToya, live in the Atlanta, Georgia area.

- Author of *Family Scars, Protect Her Heart, Exhausted Cries,* and *How to Climb the Mountains of Financial Aid*
- Winner of a national radio show essay contest
- Higher Education professional and visionary leader
- Capricorn, loves New Jack Swing music

If you would like to contact the author, email him at campaniapublishing@gmail.com

For the latest news and information, please go onto www.traejohnson.com. Please click the subscribe button so you can receive emails and newsletters.

Made in the USA
Columbia, SC
15 January 2021